It wasn't unt Valerie reme~~~~ **the night in a small space—together.**

Had it crossed Owen's mind as well? They were both adults, so they could handle the situation. She had no doubt Owen would be considerate and would never apply pressure to do anything she didn't want. The puzzling part had become her wanting more than she should.

Owen followed her up to the porch. She waited as he unlocked the door then allowed her to go in first. They stood in the living area for a moment as if unsure about what to do next.

He cleared his throat. "It's a little cool in here. I think I'll turn on the fire."

Soon the gas logs were glowing.

Her hands shook slightly. She could have been on her first date for how nervous she acted around him. What was happening between them? Despite having a crush on him for years, she'd never felt this sexual attraction she did this evening. It stimulated her and scared her at the same time. The right thing to do would be not to act on it.

Dear Reader,

This book is my first trip into writing an older couple. I thoroughly enjoyed it. There will be more of them in my future. This is also my third book in the Atlanta Children's Hospital series and might be my favorite.

My characters, Valerie and Owen, are old enough to know what they want, which becomes part of their problem. Sometimes we become so set in our ways we have a hard time accepting change. No matter our age, we can still grow and find love.

I hope you enjoy this story. I always love to hear from my readers. You can contact me at susancarlisle.com.

Happy reading,

Susan

WEDDING DATE WITH HER BEST FRIEND

SUSAN CARLISLE

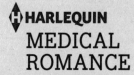

HARLEQUIN
MEDICAL
ROMANCE

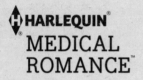

HARLEQUIN®
MEDICAL
ROMANCE™

Recycling programs
for this product may
not exist in your area.

ISBN-13: 978-1-335-59497-6

Wedding Date with Her Best Friend

Copyright © 2023 by Susan Carlisle

Harlequin Enterprises ULC
22 Adelaide St. West, 41st Floor
Toronto, Ontario M5H 4E3, Canada
www.Harlequin.com

Printed in U.S.A.

Susan Carlisle's love affair with books began when she made a bad grade in mathematics. Not allowed to watch TV until the grade had improved, she filled her time with books. Turning her love of reading into a love for writing romance, she pens hot medicals. She loves castles, traveling, afternoon tea, reading voraciously and hearing from her readers. Join her newsletter at susancarlisle.com.

Books by Susan Carlisle

Harlequin Medical Romance

Atlanta Children's Hospital

Mending the ER Doc's Heart
Reunited with the Children's Doc

Miracles in the Making

The Neonatal Doc's Baby Surprise

Pacific Paradise, Second Chance
The Single Dad's Holiday Wish
Reunited with Her Daredevil Doc
Taming the Hot-Shot Doc
From Florida Fling to Forever

Visit the Author Profile page
at Harlequin.com for more titles.

To Thomas.
May May loves you.

**Praise for
Susan Carlisle**

CHAPTER ONE

THAT FLUTTER TRAVELED through Valerie Hughes when Owen Clifton entered the break room. She pushed down the awareness of him she always felt when he came near. This time was no different. She had no intention of getting involved with him even if he were emotionally available, which he wasn't. She shifted in the metal chair as she returned her paper cup to the table in front of her.

"Hey, Valerie." A smile formed on Owen's lips as he made his way toward her with a plastic container in his hand. They shared an addiction to sweets. She had no doubt there would be a treat worth eating inside the semi-clear plastic box. More than once they'd caught up in the break room over a candy bar. That's how they had become such good friends.

"I see one of your admirers brought you something." She indicated the container with a nod of her head.

"Uh, what? Oh, yeah. Lisa brought me a thank-you gift for helping her out."

Valerie grinned. He did that type of thing all the time. Always helping someone. He had no idea the effect he had on women. Almost every single female in the department had brought him something special to eat at one time or another. What made it so humorous was he had no idea they were flirting with him. Time and again she'd seen it happen.

She had been working at Atlanta Children's Hospital in the anesthesia department for six years. Owen had already been on staff when she'd joined; he was a recent widower. Being one of those men who grew better looking with age and having an engaging personality, the women in the department flocked to him. For her, more than that he was a compassionate and caring doctor. She admired him. He was nothing like the low-life man she had been involved with who not only broke her heart but had been running around on his wife.

Owen didn't look at her as he shifted the box from hand to hand. Why was he acting nervous? They'd been work friends for a long time, and good friends for almost as long. She'd never seen him like this. And she knew him well enough to know something wasn't right. He looked over his shoulder as if expecting someone. His gaze met hers again.

What was she missing? It wasn't her birthday, so it couldn't be a surprise party. Or was something going on in the hallway he was protecting her from seeing? "Is there something wrong? A problem with a patient?"

He cleared his throat. "Um, do you mind if I close the door?"

Owen sounded so unsure, which was very unlike him. Unease welled up inside her, and she sat straighter in the chair. "Of course not. You're starting to freak me out a little. What's going on?" She looked to the door and back at Owen. "Who sent you in here to talk to me?"

In the six years they had worked together, she'd never known Owen to cross the line between professional and personal. Every conversation was held in public, in front of others in the department. This wasn't done by discussion but more as a silent mutual agreement. They sometimes joined groups of coworkers for meals and parties, but never crossed the line to anything more. That suited her just fine. He seemed like a great guy, but she had been misled before by appearances.

Owen stood and shut the door then sat down, pushing a hand through dark hair that had turned white at the temples. "No one sent me. Nothing's wrong. I just have something I want to ask you, and I don't want us to be the subject of hospital gossip."

Now she was really intrigued. She faced him. "Okay. Talk away." Her words sounded lighter than she felt.

"I need a favor," he stated.

All this drama had been about a favor? The tightness in her chest completely disappeared. Through the years they had traded cases, days off and attendance at meetings. What was so special about this favor that it had to be asked in secret? What really held her attention was he'd never asked her for a personal one. She fiddled with her now-empty paper cup, twisting it, then met his look. "What kind of favor?"

"I need a date for my nephew's wedding. Will you go with me?"

Valerie's heart rate started to race. Owen was asking her out! Did he have any idea of the crush she had on him? No, she'd kept that under wraps. She'd manage her reaction carefully. Why would he be asking her out now? Owen had never even suggested he liked her more than as a colleague. She'd never known him to go out with anyone. "I, uh, hadn't expected that. Not that I'm not flattered but before I answer, can I have a few more details?"

He had the good grace to turn pink. It was cute. Apparently he was embarrassed. He looked down at his hands. "Elaine's been gone now for five years."

Valerie had no doubt he knew the months, hours and minutes since her death. Valerie had never seen or heard of a man more devoted to his wife, dead or alive. Too often Valerie had wondered what it would be like to have someone that much in love with her. She wanted a man who would be that faithful. One who would put her happiness first. Sadly, so far in her life that hadn't happened. The man she'd put her trust in, believed she would marry, certainly hadn't felt that way. He'd used her and then thrown her away like food gone bad in a refrigerator. Now she couldn't help but be leery of it happening again.

"My kids have decided I'm lonely and it's time for me to start dating."

He sounded as excited about that as he would if he were being served dirt for dinner.

"They've been trying to set me up. I've managed to fend them off, but I have a nephew who is getting married in a few weeks. They said I should have a date for this wedding, and if I don't they'd find me one."

Valerie covered her mouth to conceal a grin.

Owen glared. "It's not funny. I've heard

about some of those women online. They'd eat me alive. I haven't been on a date in twenty, no, twenty-eight years." He pulled his brows together. "Do they still call it dating?"

At that, Valerie guffawed. "It's still called dating." Not that she would really know. She hadn't been out seriously with a man in ages. At least not out and about. In her last serious "relationship," her boyfriend, Ray, had always made an excuse for them to stay in. She couldn't imagine any reason somebody wouldn't want to go out with Owen though. He was an all-around nice guy. In fact, she'd admired his attributes for a long time. Yet she hesitated to accept his proposal.

He leaned back in the chair with a disgusted look on his face. "I can't take one more phone call or nudge or surprise meeting with the unmarried parent of one the kids' friends. They've even gotten my sister-in-law and brother involved."

His frustration made Valerie's smile grow while her heart went out to him.

"I just want to shut them down. Enjoy the weekend with my family. I thought if I brought my own significant other then maybe they'd leave me alone for a while."

"So basically, you're going to be using me."

He had the good grace to give her a sheepish look. "I wish I could tell you differently, but I guess that's true. I don't know many people outside of work. I don't go to places where there are a lot of single women. I haven't been to a real party in years. I don't want to take a stranger. I like you. We're friends, so I thought of you. We respect each other and I enjoy your company. The wedding is supposed to be at a very nice resort. I thought you might like a chance to get out of town for a few days." He shrugged. "Maybe enjoy the fall leaves."

Owen was using the hard sell, saying all of the right things but leaving out that he really wanted to spend time with her. But that was too much to expect. Probably because he sensed she'd run for the hills if he did. Their friendship worked partly because they knew the other wasn't interested in anything more than friendship. She didn't dare let what happened before happen again.

"Are you sure it's a good idea to be tricking your children or leading them to believe there's something between us that's not there?"

"It's just for a few days, then I can tell them we broke up. All we have to do is share some meals together, smile and have pleasant conversations with my family. I just need them to stop pushing women at me. I'm not ready to get involved with anyone. I may never be."

There was Valerie's confirmation. At least they were on the same plane. If she didn't start to want or expect anything more, all would be good. She did want to help him out. Still, a niggle of doubt made her say, "Let me think about it."

His shoulders slumped.

"Just give me overnight. I promise to get right back to you. I may be on call." She had to admit she wanted to go. Too much. Maybe if she did, she could get over her silly crush. Those emotions she'd learned the hard way she couldn't trust.

"I already checked. You're not."

Wow, he really wanted her to go. "I need a chance to think about it. I don't want to do anything that would hurt our friendship or our work relationship."

He nodded. "It's not like we're going to be sharing a room. I'll see to it that you have our own space."

"Won't your children think that's odd?"

He twisted his lips. "They might, but I think they'll just be glad I brought someone."

A staff member pushed the door open. Owen jumped up, a guilty look covering his face. Would he wear that look the entire time if she agreed to go with him? She had no desire to have him be ashamed of her. She'd ex-

perienced that before from other men. That
had been enough.

The young nurse glanced between them.
"I've been looking for you, Dr. Clifton.
They're ready for you in OR four."

"I'm on my way." He glanced at Valerie.

"I'll let you know."

He gave her a nod then followed the smiling staff member out the door.

Owen shook his head while he made his
way to the OR. It had been years since he
had asked anyone out. At least a woman that
wasn't his wife. He couldn't say he enjoyed
it much more now than he had in his youth.
The fear of being turned down hovered around
every word.

Valerie hadn't said no. She'd just wanted
to think about it. That he could understand.
She had been as shocked as him judging by
the nervous look on her face. When he'd first
come up with the plan, he feared he might
be losing his mind. How could he do it to
Elaine? If he were out with another woman,
then it would mean that Elaine was truly gone.
It made the truth real. He worked to stop the
tremble of his hands. That wasn't the way he
wanted it.

Time went by with his kids continuing

to nudge him to start going out. Kaitlyn, his daughter, had rallied the troops to gang up on him. All the calling and cajoling had him thinking seriously about asking Valerie. Surely it would be better to invite someone he knew, who didn't expect personal involvement instead of being set up with a stranger.

He had been surprised at how eager his children had been for him to start dating. Apparently, they were worried about him, now that they were all away from home. At least Valerie hadn't turned him down right away. That would have been devastating.

But it wasn't until he'd left her that he'd come to that realization. Before talking to her, he wouldn't have thought it really mattered one way or another what her answer would be. For some reason it had become important Valerie go with him. He was comfortable with her.

He'd worked with Valerie for years and he liked her. Maybe if she did just this one thing then his children would get off his case. He would've made the effort they wanted. Still, it wasn't worth worrying over until he found out what Valerie decided.

As an adult he didn't need to prove anything to his children. Still, he wanted them to know he could take care of himself without their pushing and help. His children needed to focus on their lives.

Owen pulled on his surgical cap and stepped up to the scrubbing station. As he scrubbed up, Valerie's face came to mind. She really was an attractive woman. It wasn't until recently that he had started to notice women again. For so many years he'd kept the blinders on. He loved his wife too much to run around on her. As far as he was concerned, he was still married. Growing up, he'd seen the hurt inflicted by infidelity. His mother spent more than one night staying up late waiting on his father. The fights that followed were nasty. Owen had promised himself as a child he would never treat his wife that way. And he hadn't. He believed in honoring those he loved.

An OR nurse approached him. He held up his hands, letting her pull on his gloves. He shouldered his way through the OR doors. This procedure shouldn't take long. A three-year-old girl getting ear tubes.

"Let's get this young lady asleep and comfortable." He stepped to the head of the table. "She's in good health? No fever or issues?"

"All good, Doctor," one of the OR staff responded.

"Then here we go." Owen placed the small

rubber mask over the girl's nose and mouth. When the child was anesthetized, he moved her head to the side, making sure the airway remained clear. He positioned her head so the ears, nose and throat doctor could insert the first tube. Soon Owen was able to swap sides for the surgeon to place the second tube.

"Done," the ENT surgeon announced.

Owen backed off the gas. He placed an oxygen canula under the child's nose, then rechecked the monitors. "I'm ready for her to go to recovery."

"I'll clean up and speak to the parents." The ENT removed his mask, gown and gloves. "Thanks, Owen."

"Anytime."

Owen finished disposing of the used equipment then headed to recovery, where he joined the nurse caring for his patient. "How's she doing?"

"Well." They both glanced at the monitor.

The nurse looked at the IV placement then made a note on her electronic pad. Owen gave her his report then left the recovery room. He was on his way to the nursing station when he heard his name being called. It was Valerie.

"Owen!"

Their eyes met over their masks before her attention returned to her patient. Even dressed in blue scrubs with a scrub coat over them Valerie had an appeal he'd given little thought to before today. It was clear she had lovely curves. The unflattering clothes did little to hide them. Her surgical cap had large pink flowers on it, adding a pop of color in an otherwise monochromic space. He'd never realized how Valerie had a way of lighting up a room. Seeing her always made him smile.

He shook his head. For years he'd known her and never given her this much thought. More than once he'd asked her to help him. Since asking her to the wedding she not been far from his thoughts. She hadn't even agreed to go with him, and he'd become fixated on her. The idea made him a little sick to his stomach while at the same time gave him a buzz of excitement. All of a sudden it mattered if she went along with his plan. But what he needed to do was concentrate on his charting.

"I need help."

"What procedure did your patient have?" Owen demanded.

"Appendectomy." Valerie pressed down on the boy's incision area, her gloved hands covered in blood.

A nurse appeared at her side, tearing open a packet of padding.

"On three," Valerie said. "One, two, three." She lifted her hands, and the nurse quickly applied the absorbent material, pressing down. Valerie's hands went on top of the nurse's.

Owen listened to the boy's heart with his stethoscope. His pulse was faint, weak. "I need a bulb here."

A nurse handed him one. He placed the mask over the boy's mouth and nose and pressed in on the plastic bulb, giving the boy oxygen.

"Call Dr. Powers. Tell him we're bringing his patient back. Stat." Valerie called over her shoulder, then looked at the monitors. "BP still going down. Get fluids on board."

Another nurse arrived with the drip stand and fluid bag, then set it up.

"Take over here." The nurse applied her hands as soon as Valerie moved hers. Seconds later Valerie pushed the needle into the port.

"Eighty over fifty," Owen called.

Other staff joined them.

"Let's get him moving," Valerie said.

Owen continued to monitor the boy's heart rate as they ran alongside the gurney into the OR.

Dr. Powers rushed in as they transferred the patient onto the table. "Patient status?"

"There's a bleeder somewhere." Valerie continued the compression.

Owen squeezed the handheld ventilator at a constant pace.

"Get two packs of O in here. We need to get this child open and find that bleeder."

"Owen," Valerie said, "will you do the intubating and handle the anesthetic?"

"Sure. Intubating kit. Stat."

"Here you go." The OR nurse handed him the items as the words came out of his mouth.

Less than an hour later the problem had been found and the child stabilized. Valerie had insisted on staying at the boy's side until he was moved to the ICU. He would have one night of observation before going to a room.

Owen looked up from where he sat behind the nurses' station. Valerie stood over the boy watching while his gurney went through the door Her skin had turned pale. She looked beat. He went to her. "Hey, Valerie, are you okay?"

Her hands visibly shook. "Huh?"

He'd never seen her rattled. She was now.

"I'm fine. I'm fine. I need to clean up, then go back check on him."

Owen placed his hand on her arm. "You

need to take a moment to regroup before you do that. This isn't like you."

"I'm fine. Really, I am."

"You don't look that way. What's going on?"

Valerie offered him a weak, apologetic smile. She scanned the area as if making sure no one else was around before she eased onto the bench between the row of lockers. "I had something similar to what happened to my patient today happen when I was just starting out on my first job. It didn't end as well as it did today. I'm just a little upset. I'll have it together in a few minutes. I know it's unprofessional. It just got to me a little."

Owen sank down beside her, making sure to leave plenty of room between them. "That's understandable. We're human after all."

She gave him a weak smile. "Thanks for looking out for me."

"Not a problem."

Valerie stood. "I appreciate the pep talk."

"No problem. I've had to have plenty of pep talks in my life. It doesn't hurt to share one." Heaven knew after Elaine's death he'd been sobbing in his office more than once when his brother had come in and consoled him.

Her smile grew. For some reason that made

Owen's chest expand like he'd ridden to her rescue.

"I'm going to clean up and go make my evening rounds." She started toward the bathroom at the back of the room.

"I'll leave you to it then." Owen headed toward the door.

"Owen."

"Yes?" He stood up to face her.

"Thank you."

He nodded. "Anytime."

The next morning the surgery department hummed with staff and patients. Valerie didn't have time to do little more than prepare for her first case. She looked for Owen. Not finding him, she released a sigh of relief. She'd come close to falling apart emotionally in front of him, which was highly unprofessional. That hadn't happened in twenty years, then it did just after Owen asked her to spend a weekend with his family. Could the timing be worse?

All night long she'd rolled around in bed thinking about his weekend proposal. She had done all the "what-ifs" to see if it was a good idea to agree to the plan. After more hours than she wanted to admit, she had concluded she would go. She liked Owen and was honored he'd asked her. What could it hurt? Maybe it would help her get over her crush on him. That would be a good thing.

"Hey, Valerie."

She jumped at the deep voice that came from behind her. Owen. Her heart leaped. "Good morning."

He stepped closer. So much so she warmed. "How're you doing? I thought about you last night. I hope you got some rest."

His concern shouldn't affect her in the way it did. He was just being nice. "I'm good."

"I'm glad to hear it."

One of the nurses called his name. "Got to go. Have a good day."

It wasn't until after lunch that she saw him again.

He came to stand near her. "How's it going today? All good?"

"Yes. Thanks for your concern and help yesterday. I'm all right. You don't have to worry about me." But she had to admit she sort of liked it. Too much of her life had involved a man not caring.

"I'm not worried. Just wondering." He picked up the next day's schedule.

"I appreciate you asking. I'm just embarrassed."

His gaze met hers, the sincerity in his eyes reassuring her. "No reason to be."

Valerie studied him. She liked the white at his temples; it gave him a distinguished air. He wasn't wearing his silver wire-rimmed glasses at the moment, but she liked those on him as well. He removed them when he wasn't working. She knew him well enough to register that small detail. Despite her near emotional collapse, he put her at ease.

She glanced around. Seeing no one nearby, she met his gaze with a direct one of her own. "I've been thinking that if I agree to go to the wedding with you, we should practice being around each other outside of the hospital. Your children will never believe us otherwise."

"You're agreeing to go?"

"I thought a lot about it last night. After yesterday I owe you a favor." She hadn't been sure about it until a moment ago though. She wanted to go. Wanted to get to know Owen better.

He smiled with obvious relief. "Thank you."

"Is there a problem with us talking about it here? Do you not want anybody to know?" She didn't try to keep the note of hurt out of her voice. In her last relationship, Ray had kept her hidden away. Never wanting them to be seen together. It had taken her a while to understand why, but when it had become clear, it had been crystal clear. Even in a fake dating situation she wanted the man to stand beside her.

"No, I just didn't think either one of us would want to be a topic of gossip. Since it's just one weekend I think it'd be all right for this to remain between us." He put the schedule back on the counter.

"If that's the way you want it." She'd been humiliated before. Maybe this wedding weekend was a bad idea after all. She had no intention of going there again. But surely he wasn't ashamed of her, or he wouldn't have asked her to meet his family.

"Thanks."

He shifted on his feet as if he might run, but then settled. "You said something about us getting to know each other better. Like how?"

She shrugged. "We're supposed to know each other well enough to be dating. We should know more than the work aspect about each other. Our favorite colors. Vacation dreams. Stuff like that." As much as they gravitated toward each other at work, they never really shared deep feelings. Things that people dating would know about each other.

He didn't say anything, as if giving the idea thought, then, "Well, that sounds reasonable."

It might but he didn't sound enthusiastic about it. Yet she wasn't surprised. "I suggest if we're really going to do this, then we should spend some time together outside the hospital."

His brows rose as if that idea had never occurred to him. His insecurity showed as he stammered, "Uh, y-yeah. Okay."

Valerie found it rather adorable. The poor guy was struggling. Just how did he expect to get through an entire weekend playacting when he wasn't an actor? She had to help him. "How about we start with a simple meal at a restaurant?"

His head went to an angle as if he'd never heard of such a thing. "Okay. I'm on call tomorrow night so that's out."

"I'm on call the next." She watched him fidget with a pen.

He put the pen down with a thump. "So that leaves Friday night. Now about seven o'clock?"

"Sounds good." Too good. She wouldn't get her hopes up.

"Then I will pick you up then." Owen seemed perplexed by that idea.

Valerie gave him a pat on the arm. "I've got to get back to work."

He offered her a tentative smile as if he suddenly wasn't sure what he'd agreed to. "I'll see you Friday if not before."

"I'll be ready," Valerie said as she passed him on the way to the door.

CHAPTER TWO

FRIDAY EVENING OWEN pulled into Valerie's condo development right on time. He didn't want to appear too eager or make her think he didn't care enough to arrive on time. The problem remained that he wasn't sure which side he fell on. His pulse ran fast at the thought of spending time with a woman who wasn't his wife while reminding himself this dinner out would be necessary to convincing his children he and Valerie were a couple.

He took a parking spot in front of Valerie's building. Her condo was part of a group of two-story structures not far from the hospital. He knew of the complex because he passed it on the way to work, but he'd never been to Valerie's home. The red-brick period building had large windows. He studied the flowerbeds, shrubs and manicured lawn. Everything looked neat, orderly and proper. All of it reminded him of her personality and her work ethic.

The seasonal wreath on her front door wasn't quite what he'd expected, but he liked the touch. She didn't strike him as a froufrou sort of woman. That had been Elaine. His chest tightened. Taking a deep breath, he pushed the thought away.

What he had thought of as being a simple plan had moved past that. This going out and getting to know each other better went beyond them spending a weekend together. Somehow this seemed more personal. Real. As if they were really dating.

In fact, he wasn't sure what he had gotten himself into. When he had formulated his plan, he apparently hadn't thought it all the way through. The last time he had a date was so long ago he wasn't sure he knew what to do. He'd been married so long. He still *felt* married. A thread of guilt tugged at him. Wouldn't it be betraying Elaine if he had a good time?

It had taken him an inordinate amount of time to dress. Elaine would have laughed him. He'd never been a clothes horse, but still he couldn't decide what to wear. Eventually he had pulled on his favorite jeans, added a button-down shirt, tucked it in and added a belt, then a sport jacket. Done, he turned as if to ask Elaine's opinion. His chest tightened.

How long had it been since he'd cared how he looked? He studied himself in the mirror. His hair had strands of silver, but it was still thick. He kept it clipped short, but it needed a trim. He would get one before the wedding.

What was he doing?

He would go out to dinner tonight because he couldn't stand up Valerie, then he'd call off their appearance at the wedding. Afterward he'd straighten his children out. Tell them he'd handle his personal life.

Taking a deep breath, he slowly let it out. He exited the SUV, then made his way up the concrete walk. He didn't make it halfway before a door opened. Valerie stood there with a reassuring smile on her face. Had she been watching him? Or was she making sure she didn't have to invite him in? Maybe she'd just peeked out to see if he was there. He didn't want her to know how long it had taken him to approach her door.

"Hey." The word sounded rougher and more nervous than he intended.

"Hello. I need to get my sweater and purse." Valerie returned inside, leaving the door open.

She wore a simple floral dress. Her brown hair framed her face and fell to just above her shoulders. The majority of the time her hair remained under a surgical cap. The dress was a nice change from hospital scrubs. He couldn't stop watching her. Valerie looked lovely tonight.

Her eyes were green. Like the dark jade of summer leaves. Why hadn't he ever noticed that before? As she reappeared, he appreciated her curves; mature ones that she'd maintained well. Wow, he hadn't had that thought about a woman in a long time, and certainly not about Valerie. What was happening to him? His reaction to her was so out of character.

Still, he couldn't understand why he hadn't noticed all this before. Could it be because he'd been so focused on himself? That idea wasn't a comfortable one. The urge to run consumed him, but he held steady as she turned off the hall light, leaving a lone lamp on.

"I'm ready." She patted her hair.

Was Valerie as nervous as he was? Why would she be? "Uh, yeah. Let's go. I hope you're hungry." When she paused to lock the door, he waited on the walk then led her to his vehicle.

"How are you, Owen?"

"I'm fine."

"Are you sure?" She studied him. "You look a little green."

His throat tightened. Was it that obvious how uptight he was? "It's the first time I've been out with a woman in years. I'm not sure I know how to do this."

Her face turned curious. "Have dinner with a friend?"

Some of his anxiety ebbed away. "More like a female friend."

"I understand. Let's go get something to eat and enjoy ourselves. What do you say?"

"I can do that."

He saw her into the passenger seat and climbed behind the steering wheel. "I hope you like the restaurant. I've always thought it was good."

"You go there often?"

"Yes, I guess I have." It was Elaine's favorite place. In truth he hadn't been out to eat much since she'd died. Or to a party. A movie or anything that might involve couples. It was just too painful. "On second thought, I think you should pick where we go. Got any ideas?"

Valerie took a seat at the table for two outside the bistro in Decatur. The sky had turned to orange in the west as a light breeze ruffled the leaves of the tree above her head. The sound of traffic was muffled by the two blocks of buildings creating the square.

She hadn't been to this bistro before and had always wanted to try it. She hoped the relaxed atmosphere would lessen Owen's anxiety. He seemed as tight as a wound-up rubber band. The amount of time he had spent sitting in his car before coming to her door had been a clue. He had even admitted to being nervous. She'd give him positive points for that.

When she had asked where they were going to dinner, the odd look on his face and the length of time it took him to answer had been telling. Her best guess had been he'd planned to take her to his and his wife's usual place then thought better of it.

There it was again. He got another point for that. Progress.

She had no idea when she suggested them getting to know each other on a more personal level it would be so difficult for him. A couple of times she thought about letting him off the hook. Yet he'd been the one who had put all this into motion. Owen needed her help. His children were right. He needed to move on.

Their friendship had been based on the superficial things in life. Patients, their shared sweet tooth, the other staff members... They'd always held back on talking about their hopes and dreams, places they'd like to travel to, what they *really* wanted out of life. She'd been

afraid to that with him. Had it been the same
for him? Now this crazy weekend wedding
plan left them no choice but to open up. But
she would only go so far. Some things Owen
didn't need to know about.

Still, if tonight didn't go well, she'd call off
the weekend. There would be no point in them
going any further. All the same, she found it
endearing that a man so controlled in the OR
was so out of sorts around her. That he had
such strong ties to his loved ones and cared
about his children enough that he was prepared to do this to make them happy. Even if
it was for appearances only.

Owen looked up from the drinks menu. He
looked around. "This is really nice."

"I've always wanted to try this place. I hope
the food is good."

Valerie couldn't suppress the little burst of
joy that he acted as if he were relaxing some.

The waitress came to the table to take their
drink orders.

"Where did you learn about this place?"
Owen put his menu on the table.

"A couple of the nurses told me about it."
She placed her menu on top of his.

He leaned back. A horrified look crossed
his features. "You told them we were coming here?"

Valerie didn't care for the note of concern in his voice. "No. I was just listening to them talk about places they liked to go. Would it have mattered if I had told them?"

"No. Yes. I don't know." His eyes pleaded. "I'm just not ready to be the talk of the OR. I had enough of the whispered concern when my wife died. I don't want to do that to you."

He was worried about her? Her heart softened. But hadn't she heard that from another source? And it had been him covering up his lies. "I'm a big girl. I can take care of myself."

"I know, but I don't want to be the reason you're the discussion at the coffee machine."

Surely he wasn't ashamed to have her be seen with him. After all, he was the one who asked her to the wedding. Yet that would just be his family. Not the people he worked with every day.

The waitress returned with their drinks and took their orders.

Owen took a long draw on his drink. "I'll say I appreciate the service."

Valerie smiled. They were back to talking about nonpersonal, safe subjects. It was time to shake him up again. She put her elbows on the table, clasped her hands together and rested her chin on her hands. "So, Dr. Clifton, tell me one of your dirty secrets."

Owen blinked and he swallowed hard.

She fixed him with a look that didn't waver.

He took the bait and met her head-on. "Where do you want me to start?"

"Wherever you want to." Valerie continued to watch him.

Owen took a deep breath, as if he planned to tell her something of super importance. "I smoked behind my grandfather's barn when I was seven."

A laugh burst from her. "That was good. Now, tell me about your family."

He grinned. "You don't waste any time, do you?"

"No. I figure we have a whole lot of personal stuff to learn about each other." At his wince she said, "Why don't I go first." She smiled at the look of relief on his face. "I was born in Chicago. You know I have a brother and two sisters. I've talked about them before. But you might not remember my brother lives out in California. I don't see him much, but I talk to him often. One of my sisters still live in Chicago. The other lives in Louisiana. They have children. Mostly all teenagers now."

"You're a good aunt. I've heard you talking about what to buy as presents for their birthdays." His gaze had turned intent as if he were remembering a scene in his head.

"I spoil them all whenever I can." Valerie grinned. She loved doing it. They were a nice replacement for the children she didn't have.

"They're just a little younger than my children."

"Yes." Was he wondering if she would get on with his children? Or wondering why she didn't have any of her own.

"I know you went to Texas A&M to medical school then worked at Houston Children's, but you've never said what made you decide to move here."

Valerie didn't much want to talk about that time in her life. She would tell him the surface information and let that be it. "Owen, I do believe you are getting into the spirit of things. You asked a question."

He twisted his lips. "Maybe I am. Answer my question."

"I wanted a change." She raised her hands. "And here I am. I really like Atlanta, and I don't think I'll be leaving."

"A change? Any particular reason why?"

She had his interest now. But not for a reason she was comfortable with. She didn't want to talk about that time. Not even with Owen. "Let's just say it had become awkward at work and it was time to move on."

"I see." His eyes had clouded with concern.

She doubted he did. Did he know what it was to love someone and learn they had been deceiving you? She'd had to get away. From the gossip, the despair, the humiliation, the breaking of her heart and trust. The only way for her to survive had been to move and start over. To work to regain her stability.

"So, tell me about you." Valerie crossed her arms on the table and leaned forward. She didn't want to miss a word he said.

"There's not much to tell that you don't already know."

"There has to be. There's always something to tell." She wouldn't let him get away with dodging her questions. "Why don't you start off by telling me who'll be at the wedding? You said it was your nephew getting married?"

"Yes, it's my brother Will's son."

"Where does your brother live?" Valerie hated having to pull answers out of him, but she would.

"Will lives here in town. He works for an engineering firm."

She watched as Owen sat straighter. His movements were smooth and relaxed, like an animal that knew its environment and was secure in its place in it. He took good care of himself. "Are you guys close?"

"Yes. He and Sarah really helped me out the first few months after Elaine died. I was a mess. I think you'll like Sarah."

Would Sarah like her after she found out Valerie and Owen had only been pretending to be in a relationship? "How will she feel about me being at the wedding with you?"

"She'll be pleased. She thinks it's time I start dating too." He rolled his eyes.

A tightness formed in Valerie's chest as she formed the next question. "You really don't want to do that, do you?"

He shrugged. "I don't know. I don't like to be pushed into it. I'm not sure I'm ready. But I don't like my children worrying about me. And, heck, I'm just plain out of practice."

"You seem to be doing a pretty good job tonight." She gave him her best encouraging smile.

He looked at her for the first time that night with warm eyes. "I know you and like you, so it makes it easy."

Heat flowed through her. Valerie had to watch it or this man would charm her into doing something she shouldn't. "Thank you."

The waitress returned with their dinner orders. They concentrated on their meals for a while.

"I know your children's names and a few

things about them from you talking about them at work, but give me a refresher."

Owen took a long draw on his iced tea. He really didn't enjoy talking about himself. He feared Valerie might see behind the "okay" facade he'd built over the last few years. He gulped. Where had that come from? Until tonight he'd thought he'd been doing fine.

He had been wrong. This evening with Valerie proved how backward his life had turned. From his dressing to please his wife, to the feeling of guilt he carried, right up to not wanting anyone they knew to see them together. Valerie having dinner with him had eaten away at the floodgates holding back years of pent-up emotion.

Owen got a momentary reprieve when the waitress returned with a refill of their drinks.

Valerie gave him a sympathetic look. "You know we don't have to do this if you don't want to."

Did she want out of their agreement or was she being nice enough to offer him the chance. "I don't mind."

"Well, you could've fooled me."

He leaned forward, placing his elbows on the table. She returned his gaze without a blink. "I know I'm acting like I'm not having a good time. But I assure you I am not having a bad one." He waved his hand around. "I just haven't done this in a long time."

"You keep saying that. Why haven't you done it?"

His gaze held hers. He wasn't going to tell her he felt disloyal to his dead wife. How crazy did that sound? He was uncomfortable having a good time and disappointed in letting Valerie down There was no winning. "I guess I just haven't wanted to."

She placed a hand on his. Hers was warm, soft and reassuring. "We're just talking. One friend to another."

Valerie was his friend. They'd been working together for years. All he had to do was think of her as a colleague again. Why was he even letting thoughts of her as a woman enter his mind? As long as he kept her in the right spot in his head, then he'd be okay.

"Hey, I don't expect anything. Nothing more than you can give. Now, will you tell me about your children?"

Owen took a deep breath. He could do that. He was a proud, doting father. "Kaitlyn is the oldest. She's married and lives in Marietta."

"Yes, I remember you talking about her wedding."

"Yeah. I don't see her so often, despite how close she lives. She does something with computers, and her husband works in the city engineering department. They both are busy people. She's the one who rallied the troops to convince me I need to go out. The boys will agree to anything just to get her to hush."

Valerie nodded as she continued to watch him.

"Rich is my middle child. He is tall and thoughtful and the most like his mother, yet he has a powerful personality. He's finishing college and thinking about medical school. I'm trying not to influence his decision. He has a girlfriend. She's a nice girl. I expect they'll marry when she finishes school."

Owen had to admit he needed to talk. Living alone had done him no favors in that regard. Just to have a conversation with someone who listened and showed interest in his life. He'd missed the give and take of talking to someone.

"John's your youngest, isn't he? He's the one who just started college."

"Yep. He made me an empty nester, but he comes home more than the others. So I get to see him pretty often."

The waitress interrupted them to take their dessert order.

As they ate their desserts, Owen's attention settled on Valerie's lips. Why was he only just noticing how soft and plump they looked? He'd seen her with colleagues, patients and their family members and never noticed her lips before. She'd always had something about her that put them at ease. Just as he was around her. Valerie really cared about people, him. Subconsciously he must have been noticing her more than he realized. He liked it when she'd talked about her nieces and nephews. Her face lit up. She liked children. That had been one of the things that had run through his mind when thinking about going out with someone, before quickly discarding the idea. He was a man with three children after all.

After paying for the meal, he escorted her toward the door. When a customer stood up quickly, pushing out his chair in front of Valerie, she stopped. Owen placed a hand at the small of her back to steady her. His hand tingled at the contact. The man apologized, and Valerie moved past him. Owen missed the contact between them, yet his heart still continued to race. This wasn't the reaction he wanted or expected.

Valerie continued to weave between the tables and chairs, Owen following as she made her way to his SUV.

There Valerie faced him. "Owen, thank you for the nice time tonight."

"I enjoyed it."

Her eyes widened, and she tilted her head as if she questioned that statement.

"Don't look so surprised."

"I have to admit I am. During most of it you looked like you might run at any second."

Owen chest tightened. He didn't like the idea of her not believing he'd appreciated her company. "I know I bumbled my way through most of it."

She placed her hand on his forearm. He immediately felt the reassuring heat. "Hey, nobody said there were any rules."

"Thank you. So do you think it'll work out for a weekend away?"

She removed her hand then gave him a firm nod. "I think we can make it work."

The ring of his phone stopped their conversation. He answered. "Yeah, I'm on my way. I'll be there in about ten minutes."

He had hardly ended his call when the ring tone sounded on Valerie's phone "Yes. I'm on my way."

"Apparently this isn't the usual emergency. They need both of us." Valerie climbed into the car.

Owen got behind the wheel, and they headed out of the parking lot.

Valerie sat with her hands clasped in her

lap. "The nurse said something about a major automobile accident."

"Sounds like we have a night ahead of us." Owen turned into the hospital parking lot.

Without a word they climbed out of the car and headed for the staff door, up to the second floor to the surgery department then into the locker room. A couple of the staff members' eyes widened when they entered together, obviously dressed for dinner, yet no one made a comment.

As Owen went to his locker Valerie said, "I'll see you in there."

Less than five minutes later they met again in the surgical scrub area. Both were dressed in mint green scrubs, and Owen stood beside her as they sanitized their hands. Valerie already wore a mask. He marveled at her emerald eyes, which reminded him of fresh grass in the spring.

She wore one of her kid print surgical caps to cover her hair, but he much preferred the look of it down and flowing around her shoulders. Whoa, that was a wayward thought. They'd had a simple dinner, and his thoughts made him feel like a man smitten by a woman. That had to stop. They had a friendship between them and that was it. He couldn't handle anything more.

Valerie met his look. "Is there a problem?"

"No." Panic rippled through him. He'd been caught staring. "Thank you for coming to dinner."

Her smile reached eyes that glowed. "You are welcome."

He had the good grace to look ashamed. "I can't say it was the easiest thing I've done. But I also have to admit that it was nice to have somebody to talk to outside the hospital."

Her mouth took quirked. "Thank you, I think."

He stepped closer. "Really, despite all appearances, I had a good time."

A nurse came in through the side door. "Ready for gloves doctors?"

"Yep." Valerie held up her hands letting the scrub nurse help her. When she was finished with Valerie, the nurse turned to Owen.

"Which OR?" Owen asked.

"Number five," the nurse stated. "By the way, it's going to be a tough one. Dr. Horton is on his way along with Dr. Wilson. The gastro guy has been called in as well. The rest of the staff should be here in just a few minutes."

"What happened?" Valerie asked over her shoulder as she headed toward the OR door.

"The kid took a hit from an SUV with his motorcycle. The SUV won. He's got internal injuries. And a number of broken bones." The nurse followed them.

"Sounds like a long night ahead," Valerie said with resignation and determination.

Their assistants were already at the operating table. Owen stood beside Valerie as they listened to the report on the patient from the ER doctor. They had just finished when Dr. Horton entered the room.

"Someone tell me what we've got here."

One of the ER staff spoke up. "Boy's motorcycle collided with an automobile. He's got a broken femur, a broken arm and there's internal bleeding."

"Let's go in and get the bleeding under control before Ortho and Plastic show up to see what they can do tonight." He lifted a large pressure bandage from the boy's abdomen. "Suction."

Owen and Valerie moved quickly into position near the patient's head.

"I'll see to blood," Valerie announced, not waiting on him to answer before she went to work.

Owen stepped to the end of the table. There he double-checked the anesthesia setup, making sure the mask was secure to the patient's face. "If you get tired, we can swap if we need to."

Valerie nodded then took a seat on the rolling stool. She asked the nurse, "Has the request for blood been called in?"

"It's on the way," Mark, one of the newer interns, said. She glanced his way. "I hadn't expected you to be called in too."

"I was still here when the boy came in. I thought I'd hang around in case you guys needed help."

"That's good of you." Her attention turned to the patient.

Owen was surprised to see Mark as well. The intern offered his help, and Owen would take it. His focus went to the machine beside him as he reviewed the numbers. He spoke to Dr. Horton in particular and the group in general. "The patient is sedated. We're ready when you are."

As the hours ticked by, Owen kept vigil on the patient's heart rate and rhythm, breathing, BP, and checked his body temp and fluid balance while the surgeon worked. Every so often Owen would rub the back of the patient's head and beneath his shoulder blades to keep circulation moving to help prevent pressure sores.

Once during the long hours Mark offered Valerie a break, and she took it. She returned and did the same for Owen.

The OR door opened. Dr. Wilson, the orthopedic surgeon, entered. He did what he could until the swelling went down. The boy also needed some time to recover from the internal surgery. The young man would have many more surgeries to come.

An alarm went off.

"Give me the numbers," Dr. Horton demanded.

Valerie called out vitals. Her voice held a tight note, but remained even and sure. Owen turned off the high, loud squeal as he reviewed the lines on the monitor.

"Let's get this boy stabilized and out of here. The rest will have to wait," Dr. Horton said to the orthopedic surgeon.

It was nearly 5:00 a.m. when Owen and Valerie escorted the patient to recovery and another hour before they handed the boy off to the ICU doctors and nurses. Afterward, they walked up the long quiet hall toward the surgery suite.

As they went by the OR they'd just been in, Mark exited. He looked surprised to see them but soon recovered. "Night, y'all. I mean, mornin'." He grinned and kept moving down the hall.

"I would've thought he'd have been long gone." Valerie glanced back at Mark.

"He must have gotten caught up in helping

straighten the OR. Nice guy. Eager to learn." Owen pulled his head covering off. "That's a night I don't hope to repeat."

"Hey, we still have reports to give." Valerie yawned.

She pushed the door to the dictation room open. Taking a seat, she went to work. Owen did the same. Valerie finished before him, giving him a wave as she left the room.

Five minutes later he found her in the locker room. She'd changed out of her scrubs back into the clothes she'd worn to dinner.

"I'll be ready to go in a few minutes to take you—"

A couple of doctors entered the room, coming to work for the morning surgeries. By the look of interest on their faces, they had heard what he had said. Horror washed through him. The one thing Owen didn't want to have happen was the rumor to get out he and Valerie were involved.

She must have seen his reaction. The joy left her eyes. She glanced at the doctors as they moved into another part of the locker room. Her mouth formed a thin line. "I'll wait for you near the staff door."

He blinked. He'd mess up. "Valerie—"

"I'm tired, Owen. I'm ready to go home to

a hot shower and bed." She opened the door to the hall.

Owen grabbed his wallet and keys, leaving his dinner clothes in his locker for later and hurried after Valerie. When he joined her, she pushed through the door and walked to his SUV without saying a word.

Moments later Owen pulled out of the parking lot. "Valerie, I'm sorry I acted like we'd just gotten caught in a compromising situation. I'm just sensitive to gossip. Too often after Elaine died, I was the topic of conversation."

"It's okay. I get it. Maybe someone else is better suited to go to the wedding with you. There're any number of the women in surgery who would go with you. Maybe you should ask one of them."

Owen glanced at her. "I'm sorry. I didn't mean to act that way."

"Let's just not talk about it anymore. I'm tired and want to go home."

He had to fix this. They had been friends before he suggested she help him. He wanted to keep that.

CHAPTER THREE

TWO DAYS LATER the morning light was just reaching around the buildings when Valerie entered the hospital. She'd spent most of the day before in bed after her long night in the OR. The rest of the day she did her chores and read.

Far too often Owen slipped into her thoughts. She'd already had a man in her life who acted ashamed of her. Worse than that, he'd lied and humiliated her. To discover he had been cheating on his wife with her had been the ultimate betrayal. He had been a visiting doctor, and she'd been swept off her feet. Nothing good had come out of it. She had no desire to experience that again, not even with someone she'd had a crush on for years. Owen obviously didn't want people to know they had been out together. And that hurt. Too much.

All too in her life she'd loved someone who didn't love her back. First it was her father leaving her family when she was five. When her mother remarried her stepfather, he barely tolerated her. Valerie's brother and sisters were already out of the house, leaving her to take most of the stepfather's verbal abuse. Valerie had no intentions of being drawn in by feelings she couldn't trust. She intended to tell Owen he needed to find someone else to help him keep his children at bay.

Making her way to the floor where her patients waited for surgery, she prepared for a quick visit to reassure them since she hadn't been there to do it the night before. She loved this hospital and her patients. She was happy here. When she'd moved to this metropolitan hospital, she feared she might be overwhelmed but instead she'd found her home.

She spoke to a number of the staff as she made her way to the nurses' station. Being a part of helping children filled her need to give. Here she was appreciated and useful. As an anesthesiologist she had little ongoing interaction with patients, yet she took great pride in knowing she had helped patients handle the pain of surgery.

Wearing only her dark blue scrubs, with her stethoscope around her neck, she checked in at the nurses' station and picked up her list of patients and their room numbers. She pulled her glasses from where they hung in the V of her shirt. Slipping them on, she studied the list.

She had purposely left her white lab coat behind. Many adolescent patients had white coat phobia. Especially the chronically ill ones. What the patient and family faced was traumatic enough without adding more uncertainly.

Owen joined her at the desk. "Mornin', Valerie."

"Hey, Owen."

"You recovered from the all-nighter, I hope."

She glanced at him. After the way they had left things the other night, he sure acted friendly. "Yep. I got plenty of rest yesterday."

"I'm glad to hear it. What kind of schedule do you have today?"

"It's pretty full. Especially since I didn't get to visit my patients last night. I've got to get to it this morning." Valerie studied the paperwork in front of her.

"That's right, you like to visit them in the evenings, don't you?"

She blinked. Owen had paid that much attention to her schedule, her routine. They were friends. He'd noticed her habits. Maybe she was being too hard on him. Maybe her expectations were too high, even unrealistic. He didn't know her background because she hadn't wanted to share it. Therefore, she couldn't blame him for something he didn't know anything about. "Yes, I like to visit in the evening. It always seemed harsh to me just to pop in in the morning and say, hey, I'm going to put you to sleep and then leave. Then they don't see you again until they wake in recovery and that's for only a couple of seconds."

"You're right. I hadn't thought of it that way. I may change my method."

"Part of our job is reassuring the patient. I don't think that necessarily happens in just three minutes of conversation."

His gaze met hers. "That's one of the things I admire about you. You really are so patient aware."

It was nice to have Owen confirm her belief, especially one so important to her.

"Do you think—" he looked around "—we could talk for a few minutes? I want to apologize for how things were left the other night."

"No apology necessary." She didn't want to go into it. They had a great friendship, and she wanted to keep it at that.

"I think there is. I value our friendship, but I'm selfish enough to beg for your help on the wedding weekend. I couldn't do it with anyone else. What can I do to convince you to help me?"

He sounded so pitiful and earnest her hackles lowered. "Look, I can't talk about it right now. I've got patients to see. Maybe when we're both done this afternoon."

Owen put up a hand. "Okay, okay. You're right. We both have people waiting on us. I'll check in with you later."

Valerie watched him stroll down the hall. She shook her head. Why did she have to have a soft spot for Owen of all people? She feared getting into a tangled web she might not be able to get out of. At least not with her heart intact. She hadn't noticed another man after meeting Owen, and the issue only became worse when she found out he was available. If she seriously considered his crazy idea for the weekend, she had to control her feelings for him. Those same feelings that had gotten her in trouble last time. Maybe spending more personal time outside of the hospital would help her squash those emotions from her mind and heart.

Valerie huffed. At forty-two, she was too old for all this nonsense, but she was going to play along for him. Picking up the tech pad, she headed toward her first patient's room.

Later that afternoon she went in search of

Owen. She found him in the small room that was his office. She tapped on the door. At the sound of his voice, she entered. She closed the door behind her and took the only empty chair in the tiny space. "All right, tell me what's expected of me on this wedding weekend."

A look of surprise came over Owen's face as if he'd been taken off guard by her arrival. He recovered well, leaning causally back in his desk chair. Crossing his arms across his chest, he said, "We'll drive up to Blue Ridge. I mentioned that the wedding is at a resort. My brother and sister-in-law have rented a lodge and cabins there."

"Is everyone staying together?"

"Yes and no. It's a large resort. The cabins are on the property. All the events, I guess, take place at the lodge, but we would be staying in a cabin."

"Your children will be staying in the cabin with us?"

He shook his head. Thank goodness that wasn't going to happen. "No, my children are in the wedding and will be staying in the lodge with the wedding party."

Relief washed over her. Maybe it would be easier to get though a weekend with Owen if his children weren't watching over them all the time.

"We'll have separate sleeping arrangements," he quickly added. "I want you to feel as comfortable as possible."

"While we mislead your family." Valerie hated lying. She'd lived a lie and nothing but hurt had come out of it.

Owen winced. "It sounds dishonest when put like that." His look met hers. "I just want them to be happy. To live their own lives. Stop worrying about me."

"Have you considered talking to them?"

"I have. Sort of, but my daughter is determined. She and her brothers in the cause. They aren't listening."

"Then I guess we need to prove to them that you're a happy, well-adjusted man who's out on the prowl again."

He scowled. "I wouldn't exactly put it that way."

She smiled at his discomfort. "Okay, maybe that was overdescribing it some. I still think we need to get to know more about each other. I don't know that much about you outside of the hospital. I'm afraid they'll ask questions I can't answer. I also think I should be able to recognize them. Wouldn't they think it strange that I haven't seen a picture of them?"

"I have some pictures on my phone." Owen dug into his pocket. He scrolled through trying to find ones that might show his kids. "All of these are so old. I can't believe I don't have more recent ones. What you need to do is come to the house. I have some that were taken the last time we were all together."

"I'd like to see them. Also, where you live. If we were in a real relationship, I think I'd have been to your house."

"Then let's make it happen."

At the ring of the doorbell, Owen hurried to the front door with relief. The catering service had delivered the meal on time. The young man handed him a large box, and Owen gave him a tip before sending him on his way. He expected Valerie to arrive any moment. If anything, she was punctual.

He had gone out on a limb, an emotionally shaky one, when he had invited her to his house. Looking around his kitchen, he felt a prick of dishonesty slither through him. This had been Elaine's domain. Everything about the space captured Elaine's personality: from the pale green walls to the butcher block island that she'd insisted they needed, to the white table and bank of windows along the back of the space. Even the knickknacks she'd placed on the top shelf of the cabinets watched over the room with the black-and-white-tile floors.

He hadn't added a new utensil since her death. It was all there waiting for her to return, despite him knowing she never would.

And he had invited another woman into Elaine's world. What had he been thinking? Valerie was a friend, a trusted one. He liked her. She wanted to know about him and his family. What better way than for her to see where he lived, and his children grew up. He could get through this.

He pulled containers out of the box, placing them in the oven to warm. He just managed to throw the delivery box out in the carport when the front doorbell rang. Quickly wiping his hands on a towel, he hurried through the house. He opened the door. Valerie stood on the stoop studying his house.

Her hair hung loose around her shoulders. He enjoyed the sight as much tonight as he had the other time. He resisted touching it. Was it as soft as it appeared? She wore a simple shirt that flowed around her. Slim jeans covered her shapely legs, and black flat shoes were on her feet. She looked casual, comfortable, completely at ease with her world.

Owen hesitated a moment, staring. Had he bitten off more than he could chew by inviting her to his home? He wanted her to know more about him so they would be able to carry off their weekend together, but this could be going too far.

"Are you going to invite me in?" she asked sweetly, her tone revealing a note of humor.

"Oh, yeah, yeah, yeah." He opened the door wider and stepped back.

"You have a nice home, Owen. Just what I thought you'd live in." She smiled and came into the hall leading to the back of the house.

Owen wasn't sure if her statement was intended as praise or not.

"Sorry I'm late. They had a drug count just as I was headed out the door. Something about the counts lately have been off."

The stealing of drugs was deplorable. He had no use for people who did that. "Great. That means we'll be under scrutiny for a while. We'll have to count and recount."

"I never have understood going into medicine with all those years of study to throw it away on taking or stealing drugs."

"I agree. Come this way. We are going to eat in the kitchen if that's okay?" He started down the hallway again. "I hope they find who it is quick."

He watched Valerie as she looked around, studying everything. He was in no doubt she didn't miss a detail. He wasn't sure he liked being so closely scrutinized. What could she be learning about him that he didn't want her to know? Owen shook his head. Did it really matter? Was there anything? After all, they were friends.

"Wow, what a nice kitchen." Valerie walked round the space, her fingers drifting along the butcher block. "I love all the windows. The afternoon light makes it look so warm and homey. My condo doesn't allow for such natural light."

Owen didn't miss the note of wistfulness in her voice. He had never thought about it. It had been what Elaine wanted, and he'd seen to it she got it.

"I'm glad we're eating here instead of some stuffy room." She looked at him, eyes wide with distress. "I'm sorry. I shouldn't have said that. I'm sure none of the rooms in this house are stuffy."

He chuckled. Something he found he did more around her than he did others. "I'm glad to hear it. Our formal dining room is rather stuffy. If it weren't for the cleaning lady, the dust would never be removed in there. It's rarely used. The only time it's put to use is on holidays or when the kids come home. I spend most of my time in here and in my den."

"I see why."

"Actually, this house is too big for just me,

but I like having a place for the children to come home to."

"Wouldn't they do that wherever you are?" she asked casually, but the words held weight.

Why did she keep asking hard questions? Why did he feel the need to justify himself? "Yeah, but this is familiar. Where they grew up. Why don't you have a seat?" He directed her toward the table he'd already set for two. "The food is already warming in the oven."

She turned toward the stove. "Is there something I can do to help?"

"Nope. I've got everything under control. All I have to do is pull it out and set it on the table." Soon, he had everything arranged. "I'm not much of a cook, so I thought I'd just have it catered."

"I love to cook. Especially baking. I'd really make use of this kitchen."

"That's right. You bring all that delicious bread to the hospital. I had no idea you baked it yourself." He already learned something new about her. It was sad he'd never ask before if she baked it.

"I do."

"You're welcome to use it anytime." Owen heart fluttered. What had he been thinking? It wasn't like he was known for blurting things. The words just seemed to pop out. Valerie baking bread in his kitchen, Elaine's kitchen, was too personal.

Her brows rose in anticipation. "Do you mean it?"

He swallowed hard. "Sure. On your next day off you're welcome to it. Remind me and I'll give you the key."

Valerie shook her head. "I'd never come when you weren't here."

He'd rather she did. This idea of getting together for a weekend had become more complicated. "For tonight let's just enjoy what I've got here." Owen pulled the aluminum cover from the chicken casserole, green beans and corn. He set a plate with rolls on the table.

"This looks great." Valerie acted more relaxed in his home than he felt at the moment.

"I did manage to put something together on my own for dessert."

She leaned in to smell the food. "I'm intrigued."

Owen paused with a spoon in the air above the casserole container. "You must finish all of your supper before you can have dessert."

She laughed. "Then serve it up, please."

The sound of her humor rippled through him, filling his chest with a warmth he never expected to feel again.

"Remember my sweet tooth." She held her plate out for him to serve.

He chuckled. It felt good. "How can I forget?"

They had been eating for a few minutes when Valerie asked, "What's your favorite color?"

Owen swallowed and put down his fork. "That question came out of the blue."

She shrugged. "That's something people who are seeing each other know."

"Really? I never thought about it."

"So, what's your favorite color?" Valerie pinned him with a look as if demanding an answer.

He thought a moment. "Blue."

"I like yellow."

Owen wasn't surprised. "That figures. You're a sunny type of person."

She smiled. "Thanks. That's a nice compliment. Now you ask me something."

He looked at her. Really looked. Her face was flush from the heat of the kitchen. Her eyes had a twinkle in them along with curiosity. The lines at the corners of her eyes came from more laughter than age. Were her lips as soft as they looked? Owen shook his head clearing that thought. He'd envisioned a business meeting between friends, and this had turned into something else. Did he really want to know all this personal stuff? He had to direct the subject to more even ground. "I need to think. I want to ask the right one."

She gave him an odd look but returned to her meal.

"Mark Lewis is really doing a good job. He's the most devoted young doctor we've had in a long time."

She picked up a roll and set it on her plate. "It seems that way. He has certainly stepped in when I have needed him."

"For me as well. He should make a great doctor if he keeps this up." Owen focused on his meal.

"He should." She gave him a direct look. "You do know your children won't quiz us about Mark."

How like her to call him on the carpet. "I know, but I find it more comfortable than talking about me."

She placed her hand over his for a moment. "You don't have to go through with this wild idea of yours. My feelings aren't so fragile that I can't accept you changing your mind. Just tell them how you feel. That they need to live their lives and you'll live yours."

"I've tried and there isn't any stopping Kaitlyn. She's got my stubborn streak. I promise I'll get with the program."

"So where were we with the questions? What's your spirit animal?"

His brows rose. "What? Is that some modern age guru question?"

She laughed. "It did get you out of that sad look. After all, if you know my favorite color then I should know your spirit animal."

"Okay. That's fair. Mine would be a tiger."

"That figures." She sounded disappointed.

"What's yours?" He became determined to know.

She proudly stretched her neck. "A giraffe."

He threw his head back and laughed. Something he hadn't done in too long. "Really? I wouldn't have guessed that. Why?"

"I love the majesty of their long necks, sweet humor and the fact they look so graceful running. What's your favorite pet?"

"I'm a dog guy." This was fun.

Valerie looked around. "I haven't seen one."

"I don't have one right now. In fact, I've been thinking about getting one, but I'm not sure I want to go through all that house training, and I work long hours." That was true, but there was more to it than that. Mostly the busier he was the less time he had to think about the loss of his Elaine. Being in their house alone had no appeal.

"You do know you can adopt an older dog and work fewer hours. I know you work far more overtime than necessary."

Owen did. His problem was he didn't want to become attached. To love a dog and lose it. To have his heart torn out again. That was a chance he refused to take. "Why don't we go to the living room for coffee and dessert? My children's pictures are in there."

"Let me help you with the dishes and putting away the food." Valerie scooted her chair back.

"You're a guest but I'm going to agree. Domestic stuff, I have found, isn't my thing. I'll do the food if you'll handle the dishes." He swallowed. The dishes he and Elaine had received as wedding presents.

Over the next few minutes, they worked together to put everything away. He marveled at how smoothly they accomplished the tasks. They worked well in and out of the OR. Owen served brownies and brewed the coffee.

Valerie found herself watching Owen. He was a handsome man. Tall, slim except for a little extra weight around the middle, which did nothing to detract from his appeal. The gray in his hair only made him look more distinguished. When he finally loosened up over dinner, he had been charming. Instead of liking him less, she found she really enjoyed his company. It was a shame he was still so hung up on his wife.

He led her to the living room, placing the plate on the coffee table. She handed him one of the two mugs she carried.

Valerie studied the formal area with the light blue floral sofa. The two matching armchairs and oak tables only added to the unlived in feel. Family pictures lined the mantel. She placed her mug down and picked up a vase on the table next to the chair. After admiring it she returned it to the same spot.

Owen adjusted it an inch. Valerie watched him. Their looks met. She attention fell to the vase once more. "I'm guessing you haven't changed much since your wife died."

He looked away from her and mumbled, "Not really."

"She had excellent taste."

That seemed to ease his trepidation. "I can't take any credit for it. My wife was the decorator. It's all I've ever known."

Valerie walked to the other side of the room. "So, tell me all about these handsome people."

She pointed to the three portraits in a line along one of the living room walls.

"The girl is Kaitlyn. The oldest and ring-leader in the need to set me up. The next is Richard, but we call him Rich. He's my name-sake. Owen Richard Jr. The last is John."

Valerie studied the portraits then turned to him. "Kaitlyn's been married…a little over a year. If I remember right."

"Yep. You have a good memory."

He had been anxious and out of sorts in the days leading up to it. Valerie had worried about him going through such a happy time without his wife. "Must've been difficult for you to handle a wedding without Elaine."

Valerie didn't miss the pain that washed over his face. "I'm not sure how I got through it. It was hard but a good day. It was not only hard on me, but it was hard on the children as well."

Valerie placed her hand on his arm. Her heart went out to him. "That's understand-able. You said Rich was thinking about med school." She needed to get them back to a pos-itive note. "What will his degree be in?"

"In chemistry. Like me."

She grinned. "Apparently the apple doesn't fall far from the tree."

"Yeah, we have more in common than our

name. It often made us butt heads. Still does. Then there is John who wants to please everyone. He isn't sure what he wants to do. He thinks he wants to go into the business world." Owen shrugged. "Who knows?"

"They sound like wonderful and interesting people."

"Thank you. I'm proud of them. I just wish they didn't worry about me as much as they do. They have enough to focus on without worrying about their dad."

"Yeah, but I consider that a major sign of their love and your closeness with them." Owen somehow brought that out in her as well.

"We do have that. Thanks for pointing it out."

She took the seat at the end of the couch. He chose the overstuffed chair across from her. "My turn. It's time for me to learn something more about you."

"What would you like to know?" Valerie wasn't sure she wanted to share everything with Owen. But he deserved answers to his questions just as she did to hers. She leaned back on the couch and placed her hands in her lap.

"I don't know. How about why aren't you married?"

Easy one. Maybe he wouldn't dig any deeper. "Let's just say it's never worked out."

A winkle formed across his forehead. "No children either?"

"No." The faster she said it the easier it was to answer. Her chances had narrowed significantly.

Owen shook his head. "I don't understand why not. You're an attractive person, self-confident and have much to offer in a relationship."

That was nice to hear coming from Owen. "I could say the same about you."

"I've been married." He looked away.

She said the words quietly. "Yeah, but you haven't even been out on a date in the last five years."

Owen shifted and looked directly at her as if to put her on the defensive. "How do you know?"

Valerie shrugged. "You told me. Remember? It's been twenty-eight years since you've been on a date. Besides, the hospital grapevine is very efficient, especially where single doctors are concerned."

His face tightened. From his reaction the other day, he didn't like being talked about. "If I'd said anything."

She gave him a half smile. "Things like that get out."

"I guess you're right. But now I can say that I have been out on a date. This is the second time we've had dinner."

"I thought this was a friendly meal. Not a date." She grinned.

He had the good grace to redden. "I guess I have gotten set in my ways."

"Will you tell me about your wife?" Valerie asked softly.

He said nothing for a while. She wasn't sure he would answer her.

"Elaine was the perfect wife. We met in college. She worked to support me through school. Before I finished, we were expecting Kaitlyn. It was a struggle, but we managed. Elaine took everything as a challenge. Sometimes I wasn't sure we'd get the bills paid but somehow, she made it all work."

"She must have been a wonderful woman."

Owen continued as if she had said nothing. "She was from a small town in South Georgia and I from one in North Georgia. We met in the middle—Atlanta—at college. We planned to build this house about ten years into our marriage. It was the dream home where we were supposed to retire." He shook his head as if trying to remove the sad memories. "Then she got sick. Soon after, she was gone."

"Elaine sounds like somebody I would've liked and admired." She placed her hand over his.

He looked at her hand a moment. "Thanks, Valerie. I think she would've liked you too. Your enthusiasm over the kitchen alone would have been your common ground."

Valerie moved to the front of the chair. "I'd love to see more of your family pictures."

A phone rang in the distance.

"I need to get that. It might be the hospital or one of the kids."

Or a perfect way to get away for a moment to gather his thoughts and calm his nerves. She watched him leave the room. Had her presence and questions been too much for him?

CHAPTER FOUR

VALERIE WAITED TEN MINUTES, then went in search of Owen. She picked up the low rumble of his voice coming down a short hallway off the main one. Following that sound, she wandered in its direction. He'd said he had a den. She bet he'd gone there to talk on the phone. The more she was around Owen, the more curious she'd became about him.

She located him in a dark paneled room. A large wooden desk sat in the center of the space with a row of windows at the back. Owen stood looking out of them. To his left was a wall of shelves filled with books and pictures, including what looked like small family memorabilia. In the center was a large TV. On the other wall sat a leather sofa and a table along with a straight wooden chair that didn't encourage anyone to visit very long. This space was obviously where Owen felt most at home.

Owen turned when she stopped in the doorway. He pulled a face, giving her an apologetic look. *It's okay*, she mouthed as he returned to reassuring whoever was on the other end of the phone.

She went to the shelves, picking up a framed picture. Owen's family stood in the traditional stance for a young family. He held the smallest of the children. His wife stood beside him with her hands on the shoulders of the two other children. They each wore smiles that didn't reach their eyes. Valerie smiled.

"That was Easter over twenty years ago," Owen said from beside her so close she could make out the citrus scent of his aftershave. "Sorry about that call. My sister-in-law was filling me in on all the wedding weekend activities. She's so wound up about them I didn't have the heart to cut her off before I did."

"You're a nice guy, Owen."

He chuckled. "No, it's more like I live in fear of her. She runs her show."

"Sounds like an interesting person."

"She can be a force to be reckoned with." He took the picture from her and placed it back on the shelf.

Valerie had been afraid she done something wrong by touching his picture until he picked up another frame and handed it to her. "Here we were on vacation. It's a much happier group. This is one of my favorite pictures."

"You all look so...perfect family."

He chuckled.

It rolled through Valerie like a warm drink on a cold day, making her shiver. Owen sounded happy.

"Not exactly perfect but a family. Elaine had a way of holding us together."

Valerie studied the tall, willowy woman with blond hair. The direct opposite of her. "I can tell she enjoyed life."

He took the frame again, looking at it. "That she did."

"You still miss her." That was an understatement, but Valerie felt she needed to say something. What would it be like to have someone love her like that? Stand by her, love her so much he would not hesitate for others to know. To be the center of his world? Sadly, she was jealous of a dead woman.

Owen's look went off into the distance. "Every minute of every day."

He sounded so sad she wrapped her arms around his neck and hugged him. After a moment's hesitation, he returned the hug. How long had it been since someone other than his family had given him a hug?

Owen pulled away but didn't let go. His

gaze met hers, held. A flicker of uncertainty went through his eyes before his head lowered. His lips were gentle on hers, as if testing their texture. Her heart held a beat waiting to see if he would continue or back away.

His mouth pressed closer as his hands tightened at her waist. He tasted of coffee and the sweetness of their dessert, which was almost as pleasurable as the kiss. Her hand clutched his waist and she leaned into him wanting more. Owen was a good kisser; the experience was living up to her dreams.

The sound of footsteps registered seconds before Owen pushed her to arm's length as if she were suddenly a bad disease he was afraid to get. His hands came to her shoulders, steadying her before they dropped away.

"Hey, Dad. I'm home." A young man's voice carried into the room.

She looked at Owen. He appeared flustered as he stumbled back.

"I shouldn't have done that," he said so softly she almost missed it, but she hadn't.

The hurt of years built up, flooded Valerie. Her lips tightened. She'd dared, for a moment, believe someone wanted her. That a man would be proud she belonged to him. Owen's words were a slap in the face. The indignity and disappointment of years ago washed over her.

"Whose car is in the drive?" Moments later a tall, youthfully thin male pulled up short just inside the door of Owen's den. His eyes went wide as he looked between her and Owen.

A coolness Valerie could attribute to Owen moving farther away from her grew between them. Those old hurts began to bubble. Now many times had her ex pushed her aside? Refused to admit she existed except when he needed her?

"John. I wasn't expecting you."

Owen's son continued to watch them, curiosity making his face almost comical.

Owen gestured toward her. "John, this is Dr. Valerie Hughes. We work together at the hospital."

"Hello, Dr. Hughes." Owen's son continued to watch her with curiosity.

Valerie forced a smile. "Hi, John. It's nice to meet you."

An awkward silent settled around the room.

"I should be going." Valerie stepped toward the door. She needed to leave before her distress showed. The last thing she wanted to learn was that Owen would treat her just as her ex had.

"I'll walk you out." Owen made a stiff movement toward the door.

As she passed John she said, "Good night, John. It was nice to meet you."

Valerie didn't slow down on her way to the front door except to pick up her purse. She said nothing and neither did Owen as he followed her.

As she circled the back of her car he said, "He didn't tell me he was coming home. I'm sorry if you were uncomfortable."

"I think you were far more uncomfortable. You had nothing to be ashamed of. We were just two adults looking at pictures in your den." She wanted to stand by Owen, but he needed to let go of the past and look to the future. Even if they were a pretend couple, she wanted him to respect her and be proud of her. Was that so much to ask?

"Yeah, but he's never seen any other woman in my den but his mother."

She offered him a wry smile. "He seemed to be handling it well. Maybe you're the one who needs to get used to the idea."

Owen got into the hospital early Monday morning. He wanted to speak with Valerie before their day got started.

Could Friday night have gone worse? She

hadn't been happy when she left. He couldn't blame her. He had kissed her then acted like he was embarrassed and ashamed of her when John showed up.

John had almost caught them. Owen had acted like he was a teenager doing something wrong. Except he was an adult in his own home. There was no reason for him to have acted the way he had or for him to make Valerie believe he regretted kissing her. On the contrary, he enjoyed kissing her. Too much.

Afterward he hadn't been able to look her in the eyes. Shame filled him. And what he said to her. He hung his head. Could a grown man be more insensitive? When their gazes had met, it had been clearly visible she'd been hurt. She was due an apology. He had asked her to do him a huge favor then insulted her.

What had he been thinking? That's the problem: he hadn't. Instead, he'd been feeling. It felt too good to have a woman in his arms again. To kiss her. To have her kiss him in return. He wasn't sure he would have stopped if John hadn't interrupted them.

He just hoped she would listen to his apology. After the fiasco of Friday night, he anticipated she'd change her mind about attending the wedding. Maybe reconsidered their friendship. That kiss certainly had shifted the relationship. Suddenly it had become more important than ever that she go with him. He wanted Valerie beside him at the wedding. Still, he wouldn't blame her if she refused.

Her reaction to him backing away had been just as over the top. What had the other men in her life done to her? He would find out. If nothing else, he wanted her to feel safe with him. He wasn't sure why it mattered so much but it did.

He pushed through the swinging door of the OR suite, walking down the hall in the direction of their offices. He planned to straighten this out now. He slowed at the department desk and spoke to the clerk. "Good morning, Melissa."

"Dr. Clifton." She handed him the device that held the information on his patients for the day.

"Have you seen Dr. Hughes?"

"She's already in OR three preparing her first patient."

"Thanks." He logged into the device. Giving the list of his patients a quick review, he then hurried down the hall.

He didn't plan to interrupt a procedure, but if Valerie hadn't started yet he would have a word with her. After scrubbing and gowning up, he stepped into the operating room. Valerie was there, but the patient had not arrived. She stood with her back to the door, organizing the tubing.

"Valerie, could I speak to you for a moment outside?"

She looked over her shoulder. "Can it wait? I'm expecting the patient any moment."

"I'd really like to talk to you now." Owen hadn't noticed Mark Lewis across the room until he spoke up. "Dr. Hughes, I'll be glad to get things going."

Valerie hesitated a moment, and Owen feared she would turn him down. Then she looked at Mark. "You don't mind?"

"Not at all." The man's voice was cheerful behind his mask.

"Thanks. I appreciate that." She went out the door.

Thankfully there was no one in the scrubbing area. They could talk in private.

"Owen, this really isn't a good time."

He agreed, but he had to get this off his chest. "I'm sorry about what happened Friday night. I should've handled it better. You were hurt and I didn't want that. I'm sorry."

"You said that Friday night. I recognize rejection. I've seen it before, and I promised myself I wouldn't put myself in that position again."

Owen stepped back. Whoa, he hadn't expected that. "What brought that on?"

Her look turned contrite, as if she'd said more than she had intended. "It's nothing."

"That didn't sound like nothing to me. Where did you get that idea? I haven't rejected you. I still want you to go with me to the wedding."

"Are you going to treat me like I have the plague there as well? You kissed me for a reason. I'd like to think it's because you like me. But I don't think you've moved past your wife far enough to be having dinner with a woman much less planning to spend a weekend with her. We wouldn't fool anyone into believing we're seeing each other. You just need to talk to your children and leave me out of your madness."

"I would call it off, but John called Kaitlyn and Rich. They know about you now. I'm sure my brother and sister-in-law do as well. I'm too deep in to call it off."

"And you still want me to spend a whole weekend surrounded by your family as a couple and you can't bring yourself to touch me without feeling guilty?" She shook her head, disbelief in each movement.

"I can do better. I will do better. I promise not to hurt you again. I've put you in a bad position. I get that. Please give me another chance."

Her look bore into him. "What happened Friday night won't happen again?"

"The kiss or the denial?"

"Denial."

"I promise." He held up his hand. Would she turn down his kisses?

Her sigh came out heavy. "Then we'll give it another try. You have to loosen up though."

"I'll try. You have my word."

She made an impolite noise in her throat. "Think again. If we're going to make them believe us, then you'll have to learn to touch me. Hold my hand. Even kiss me."

Something he feared he might enjoy too much.

A staff member entered the scrub area, giving them both a curious look.

"I have a patient waiting. We'll talk about it later." Valerie left him with a determined glint in her eyes before returning to the OR.

Relief washed through Owen as he watched her go. At first, he believed he want to convince her to keep their plans for the wedding weekend to save him from his children. Now he realized he wanted the chance to spend more time with her. The chance to kiss her again. To see if he felt as alive the second time as he had the first. He smiled at the staff member as he went out the door.

Valerie had had to remind herself to focus over the last few days. Her thoughts kept returning to Owen's kiss. It was as sweet and perfect as she had imagined. Until his son had come home. For those few minutes, Owen was Owen. Not a father, a widower, a doctor, but a man who was enjoying kissing her. The moment had been perfect. So much so that it had cut like a scalpel when he had acted as if she weren't important.

She had experienced enough rejection to last a lifetime. She had hoped Owen would be different. Quickly she learned not to expect more from him. She shouldn't have let his reactions affect her so, but she hadn't expected him to rebuff her so bluntly. That part of his personality he covered well. If she was to be his plus one at the wedding, he would have to do better than he had the other night. She hadn't realized Owen's grief went so deep. She had agreed to spend the weekend with him only because she felt sorry for the position his children had put him in.

Thankfully she hadn't seen him in the last couple of days. She'd needed the break to regroup. They'd had full caseloads and were coming and going into operating rooms at different times. She only knew when he was in the department because his name appeared on the OR schedule board near the department desk. For some reason she couldn't resist looking when she came into work.

She looked down the hallway. Owen stood beside the department desk talking to two of the young staff nurses. Their smiles were those of hero worship, just a tad too bright. Then there were the giggles as they left him, his attention immediately returning to the iPad in his hands. Valerie shook her head. He had no idea how he charmed woman. He had that personality that attracted women without him even trying. She had been pulled into that net and gotten caught too.

On Wednesday, the anesthesiology department head, Dr. Dale Rhinehart, stopped her in the hall between cases. "Valerie, you're going to be needed in surgery tomorrow to help Owen. We have an abdominal aortic aneurism. I've cleared your schedule so you can help. You and Owen work well together. Get with him. The boy has been his patient since infancy. Owen can bring you up to date."

"Okay." Had Owen asked for her to assist? It was a rare thing for two anesthesiologists to be needed for a case. Interestingly, the first case had occurred so close to this one. One thing about medicine was she never knew what would happen from one day to the next.

Dr. Rhinehart continued, "You both will have earned that long weekend you have coming up."

Had Owen told him that they were going away together? No, he wouldn't have done that. He didn't want people at work to know they were seeing each other, even if it was pretend. Just as her ex had been pretending. Except Owen didn't want the gossip whereas her ex didn't want his wife to find out he was cheating. The idea still made her sick.

"Speaking of which, there's Owen. I'll leave you two to discuss the case." Dale turned toward his office.

Generally Owen offered those around him a ready smile, but today a serious look covered his face. The lift of a corner of his mouth didn't reach his eyes. A heaviness of concern filled them instead. This Owen tugged at her heart. "I understand we're going to be in the OR again together."

"Yes, difficult case ahead." He slowed so she could match his steps.

"You're familiar with this patient?"

"Very. I've put him to sleep a number of times in his life. He grew up in this hospital.

I'm just on my way to talk to him and his parents. Would you like to come along?"

"Sure. Give me a minute to do some dictation, and I'll be ready."

"Okay, I'll be in my office."

Fifteen minutes later Valerie entered Owen's office to find him studying the tech pad. She settled into the chair in the corner of the small room made tinier by Owen's presence.

He turned off the device and locked it away in his desk.

She studied him a moment. The lines around his mouth were deeper, and his eyes didn't have their usual spark. "Are you okay?"

"Yeah. Just tired. I was reviewing Rob's case."

"Rob?"

"Yes, the boy that we're going to take care of tomorrow." He pushed back from the desk.

This was the Owen she really liked. The one with the caring heart. "You must know him really well to call him by his first name."

"I do. He's a good kid and has a great family. He's been coming here since he was a baby."

"Tell me about him." She had the sense Owen needed to talk.

"His name is Rob Martin, and he's fourteen

years old. He was born with hyperplastic left heart syndrome."

Her mouth pursed. "That's a tough one."

"Yeah. He's done great, but it's taken time and fortitude. It also took three surgeries and a transplant before he was two to get there."

Valerie didn't say anything, waiting on him to get it all out.

"For years I put him to sleep every six months for his heart biopsies." He smiled. "Even once to fix a broken arm. I've gotten to know all the family well. Five months ago, Rob started having difficulty, but we couldn't figure out want the problem was. The blood work didn't even show the problem. It turns out it was endocarditis, and it's manifested itself at the point of his original surgery. The infection settled in his, aorta which as you know is the weakest part of his body. He's a tough one. And now he has this aneurysm on his aorta."

The pain in Owen's voice made Valerie want to go to him but instead she gripped the arms of the chair.

"He's been in the hospital for the last three weeks with a PICC line and antibiotics going in him. The endocarditis made his aorta blow up like a balloon. It's a wonder it hasn't burst."

"He's been on bed rest this entire time?"

"Yes." Emotion vibrated around the single word. "All patients matter, but this one is special." Owen ran a hand through his hair making the waves more pronounced. "I know we aren't supposed to get personally involved with a patient, but there are just certain ones who come along that get to you. You can't help yourself."

She never experienced that, but she could understand. In an odd way she felt like that was what he'd done with her. Owen had gotten under her skin. "Between us and Dr. Dillard, Rob will be in good hands. We'll see to it. He's the right surgeon for the case."

"I believe so too but it'll be tough. Long hours."

"Still, I'm confident we'll take good care of him." He needed the encouragement.

"That's the plan. I'm glad you were assigned to the case. We've proven we work well together."

Valerie stood. "Why don't you introduce me to Rob?"

Owen squared his shoulders then stood. "Okay."

She followed him out of the office. Walking beside him, they made their way to the elevators. Neither said anything as they entered one.

Owen glanced at her. "I haven't seen much of you lately. How have you been?"

"Fine. Just busy here. I've also been looking for dresses to wear to the wedding."

"I didn't even think about you doing that. Please let me pay for it. After all, you're doing me a favor."

She glared at him. "I will not."

Owen rolled his shoulders and took a deep breath. They had been in the OR for five hours already, and there were many more to come. Rob had been holding his own as the surgeon worked. Replacing an infected aorta took patience and a steady hand, both of which Dr. Dillard had. The operation had been as brutal as Owen had feared.

He looked at Valerie. She had been in her position as long as he had. He massaged the back of Rob's head, moving down to his shoulders and slowly under his back to his shoulder blades, going as low as he could along the boy's back.

When Valerie looked at him, he asked, "How's it going over there?"

She nodded. "Steady."

Mark, along with a few others, had come in to observe. "If you need a break, I'll be glad to fill in."

Dr. Dillard said, as he placed the tubing for the bypass machine, "If you guys want a break, this would be a good time. After we are on bypass, things will get intense." He turned his attention back to placing the tubing.

Owen looked at Valerie. Their eyes met above their masks. "You go first. Let Mark sit in for you."

Mark moved toward Valerie.

She checked the monitors then stood and stretched her back. As Mark sat on the stool Valerie had vacated, she said, "Thanks."

The operation ground on as Dr. Dillard worked in the open chest of the boy.

Owen continued to massage Rob's neck and shoulders, keeping constant watch on the monitors making sure Rob remained stable. This was a difficult surgery at best, but when the patient had been sick for months it became more difficult.

When he'd discussed the case with Dr. Dillard, he'd believed Rob had a good chance for survival. Owen hoped it would be the case. Dr. Dillard was a good surgeon, but the odds could so easily tip in the other direction.

Valerie had been very kind to Rob and his family earlier. And she'd been just as kind to him. It had been nice to have someone he could trust to talk to. Rarely did he let his feelings about his work show. Valerie had been there for him to unload on. His nerves had been on edge until she settled him.

The hours ground on. He and Valerie changed positions every couple of hours.

She remained alert, but he could tell by the slump of her shoulders that the long, tedious hours were wearing on her. Next weekend he would gift her with some time at a spa. She would have earned it.

Finally Dr. Dillard announced with satisfaction, "Well done everyone. Let's close him up and keep a close eye on him."

There was a sense of rejuvenation going through the room at the idea that they had saved a life.

Valerie stood then twisted one way then the other.

Owen glanced over. Even in the nondescript OR scrubs he could make out her feminine curves. Valerie sure had what it took to attract a man. He blinked. Where had that thought come from? Up until a couple of weeks ago he'd only thought of her as a friend, never a woman he wanted to kiss. Now he was too aware she was a woman. It had been a long time since an unrelated female had been his concern, but Valerie had moved into that position.

He spoke to her. "You go on home. I'll see Rob settled in the CICU."

"No, I'll walk with you."

Owen wasn't surprised she'd turned his offer down. In fact, he found it admirable she wanted to see the case through.

A CICU nurse was there to receive Rob. She immediately went to work overseeing the bank of pumps sending medicines into the youth's body.

Satisfied with Rob's care and pain level, Owen turned to Valerie. "I'm going to speak to his parents."

She moved toward the door. "Do you mind if I go with you?"

He appreciated the support. "Thanks. That would be nice."

They walked quietly through the dim night-time hallways to the surgical waiting room where Rob's parents were waiting to visit their son.

Both adults stood as he and Valerie entered through the glass doors. They looked as exhausted as he felt. It had been a long tense day.

"Dr. Clifton, is there a problem?" Rob's mother asked as she hurried toward them.

He held up a hand. "Rob is fine. Dr. Hughes and I just left him. His nurse is getting him settled, and you'll get to see him very soon."

"Thank goodness." The mother visibly relaxed.

Owen placed a hand briefly on her shoulder. "Dr. Dillard did a great job. I'm sure he's already been by to see you."

"He has," Rob's father said.

"Rob did as well as expected. I know you remember from the past that the first twenty-four hours are important, then getting out of ICU." He looked from mother to father.

The mother nodded. "We know only too well."

Owen gave her an encouraging smile.

Valerie stepped up beside Owen. "Rob did great. There's no reason to think he won't continue to do so."

"Dr. Hughes is right. During the night, don't hesitate to call me if you're worried." Owen looked from one parent to the other. "I mean that."

"Thank you, Dr. Clifton. Dr. Hughes." Rob's mother hugged him. She hesitated a moment, then wrapped her arms around Valerie. Valerie returned the hug.

"I'll see you tomorrow. Get some rest." Owen started toward the door with Valerie at his side.

As they returned to the OR Valerie said, "You were great with them."

"That's not hard. They're a great family. You were good with them too. Rob's mother needed your care."

"You're right. They aren't hard to care about." Valerie yawned.

"You're worn out."

Their gazes met. "No more than you must be."

"What I really am is hungry. I'd love breakfast. How about joining me at an all-night diner."

"I know something better. Why don't you come to my place, and I'll fix us some breakfast?"

He lowered his chin and studied her in amazement. "You want to cook after the day and night we've had?"

"It's just breakfast. I'll make it short and simple so we both can get to bed." Her face went beet red. "I didn't mean—"

He chuckled dryly. "I know what you meant. I'm too hungry and the diner too far away for me to turn down the offer."

"Good. I'll see you in a few minutes at my place."

Valerie wasn't sure what had made her suggest she fix a meal. It just seemed like the natural thing to do. She was too exhausted to go out to a diner. She needed to eat, and Owen did too. It was easier and faster for her just to prepare them breakfast at her place.

Valerie gathered the eggs and bacon from the refrigerator and got the bacon started. When she let Owen in the door he asked where the bathroom was; he wanted to wash up before eating. She pointed him in the direction of the hall. "Make yourself at home. The towels are fresh."

She smiled to herself. His hair was in disarray, and she could tell he'd just chucked his clothes on. He wasn't his usual put-together self. He'd been in a hurry to get to her place. Had he been afraid she'd change her mind about the meal if he didn't get there right away?

For some reason he seemed to fit in her home. They needed to know each other better, but for her they were slipping over the edge into an emotional relationship. Could he possibly feel the same? She shook her head. No. Owen was still involved with his dead wife. How could she ever compete with her? What Valerie did know was that at this rate she would get hurt. She didn't intend to spend her life being second to somebody she couldn't even compete with.

Owen returned to the kitchen with his hair

combed and shirt tucked in. He looked as attractive as ever. The only thing that could attest to their long night was the deepening of the lines around his eyes.

"What a day." He sighed. "What can I do to help, despite my less than skillful kitchen abilities."

"Want to fix the coffee? Everything is over there by the machine."

"Now, that I have experience with." He stepped around her.

The galley kitchen felt tiny with them both in it. She pulled a bowl out from under the cabinet, then pulled the flour canister toward her, being careful not to poke him in the ribs with her elbow.

He glanced over her shoulder. "What're you doing?"

"I'm making biscuits."

"I haven't had scratch biscuits since my grandmother was alive." He smacked his lips. "I can hardly wait."

She giggled. And she didn't giggle. What was happening to her having Owen in her personal life? He stood close enough to look over her shoulder. She could feel his heat.

"The only biscuits I know how to make are bap biscuits."

"Bap biscuits?" She looked at him, her mouth only inches from his.

She watched his lips move as he said, "You know, the kind that you hit against the counter and they pop open."

She laughed.

He stepped back. "That's a nice sound this early in the morning. Or anytime for that matter."

"Thank you. That was a nice thing to say." Her heart made an extra thump. She turned back to cutting butter into the flour before adding milk. Using her hands, she worked the ingredients into a dough.

Owen continued to watch her with interest. Intently enough that he made her nervous. "This is fascinating. I didn't know anybody still made biscuits like this."

"I hope they turn out good." She floured the cutting board.

"I know at this point I could probably eat a rock."

"I hope that's the last thing these taste like. I'm going to roll this dough out. Why don't you cut them out and put them on the cookie sheet while I get the eggs started and tend to the bacon."

Owen stepped back. "Hey, I told you I wasn't any good in the kitchen."

"I think if you can put someone to sleep for surgery you can handle cutting dough and placing it on a pan. It'll be your chance to learn something new."

He released a resigned sigh. "When you put it like that, I guess I'll have to."

"I knew you were a team player." She gave him a light slap on the back. "The biscuit cutter is that round metal thing with a handle. I'll get the cookie sheet and line it with parchment paper."

Valerie's look drifted to Owen as she found another bowl and added eggs and milk to it. Owen was being precise as he cut and placed the biscuits on the baking sheet, much as he was with his patients. Was he the same when making love? If so, she bet he was a wonderful lover.

She placed the eggs into the hot skillet too quickly, making them sizzle. Jerking back so she didn't get burned, she pulled the pan off the burner and turned it down. She needed to get her attention back to what she was doing. Those types of thoughts weren't what she should be having. "I hope scrambled is all right with you."

"Sounds wonderful. The biscuits are ready to go in the oven."

Valerie slid the pan in. The loud ramble of Owen's stomach drew her attention.

He gave her a sheepish look. "Sorry about that. I'm starving."

"Give me five more minutes and I'll have you fed. How about handing me a couple of plates? They're in the cabinet above your head. The silverware is in the drawer next to you."

He did as she asked. She finished cooking the eggs and bacon and put two plates of them on the table in front of two bar stools. A basket with the biscuits went in front of them. Owen took a seat and she the other. Without discussion they both ate.

Valerie looked at Owen. It was nice to share a meal with someone in her home. Especially one who obviously enjoyed the food as much as Owen did. He was already on his third biscuit.

Between bites Owen lifted his biscuit. "These are really good."

"Thank you. I pride myself on making tasty ones." It felt particularly good to have him enjoy them.

He took another bite. "You can make these for me anytime."

"You just let me know when you'd like to have some, and I'll make it happen. They're not that difficult."

He made a sound of pleasure. "My only problem is that if I eat them all the time, I'd be as large as this room."

"I doubt that. You look trim enough to me." She looked him up and down.

"Life is too short not to enjoy things. I know that too well." Owen's voice turned sad.

Once again his wife had worked herself into a happy moment.

"I'll take care of the cleaning up since you did most of the cooking." He stood and picked up his plate.

Valerie needed to walk away before she said something she might regret. "Thanks. I'm going to take you up on that. It's past time for a shower."

With her shower completed and feeling like every step she took required effort, Valerie tightened her housecoat securely at her waist as she went to the living room to see if Owen had left.

She smiled. He lay on the sofa with his head on a cushion. One of his legs stretched across the length of the sofa while the other remained on the floor. As if half of him wanted to leave while the other wanted to stay. Despite that, he looked like he belonged there. Pulling the throw off the back of the sofa, she covered him with it. He'd earned his rest.

In her bedroom, she crawled between her sheets and drifted off to sleep to the sound of Owen's soft snores.

CHAPTER FIVE

THE VIVID BLUE of the sky and the beauty of the fall day made Valerie feel glad to be alive as they drove toward the mountains. The sunshine warmed her face through the passenger window as they traveled north.

"How much farther?" She shifted in the seat.

"A couple of hours," Owen said from behind the wheel. "Take a nap if you want."

She looked out at the trees that had turned golden, red and orange. It was beautiful. "I don't want to miss this amazing view."

"You'll get plenty of it before the weekend is over."

"I don't know if that's possible." She needed this getaway.

Owen glanced at her. "Have you ever been to Blue Ridge before?"

"Once, just after I moved to Georgia. But it

was the middle of the summer. It was beautiful then, but it's amazing now."

"This is one of my favorite places in the world."

"I can understand why. Have you traveled much?" Valerie wanted to know all she could about him.

"We traveled as a family a lot before Elaine… We've done very little but get through the days since."

Valerie studied his profile. His strong jaw had tightened as he spoke. Sometimes he'd run a hand through his hair making it stick up. She itched to smooth it back into place. "Do you always judge your life by 'before Elaine' and 'after Elaine'?"

"I've never thought about it before, but yeah, I guess I do."

Valerie wanted to move away from the direction the conversation had turned. "Now that the kids are gone, do you want to travel more?"

"By myself?" The note of surprised impossibility filled his voice. He sounded appalled by the idea.

"You can travel on your own, you know!"

He shook his head. "I don't think that's for me."

"So your plan is to remain alone, by yourself, for the rest of your life and do nothing but work?" She asked the question in a teasing tone, but she meant every word. Someone needed to tell Owen it was time to move on, to live again. As a friend, it had fallen to her.

His mouth twisted as if she made him uncomfortable with her questions. "To be truthful, I hadn't thought about it."

"Maybe you should."

Owen stayed quiet. Had she said too much? It might have been the truth, but she didn't want their weekend to start off on the wrong foot. Especially since it was shaky to begin with.

At a gray stone entrance, Owen made a left turn. They drove along a tree-lined paved road that wound up a mountain, crossing over a brook twice. Dark green laurel grew low to the ground while the evergreens mingled with the bright colors of the trees that had changed color, creating a canopy over the road. The wind sent lost leaves dancing in front of them.

She gasped as the lodge came into sight. It was amazing. The two-story A-frame was built of natural wood, and the afternoon sun reflected off the smooth surfaces of glass panels. A separate wing stretched out from both sides of the main structure. In front was a manicured lawn with flower gardens bordered with stone. The look was rustic elegance in the woods. "Mercy, this place is beautiful. I could come stay here forever."

Owen chuckled. "I'd see how the weekend goes before you say something like that. You haven't felt the full force of my family yet."

"I'm sure it's going to be fine." He'd loosened a little. Right now he was doing a good job, but as they drove closer to the lodge she noticed him growing more anxious.

"I wouldn't be surprised if all three of my children are waiting for us at the door."

She watched him. "Oh, that's right! John let them know about meeting me the other night."

Owen's gaze met hers. "I'm sure they're all excited."

Valerie clasped her hands in her lap as her stomach churned. Her self-confidence had started to wane.

Owen took her hand, squeezing it. "Hey, there's no reason to be nervous. I'll run interference. Promise."

He pulled around the circular drive and stopped under the stacked stone portico. Large wooden double doors stood between them and the lies they would be telling.

"Owen, are you sure you want to do this? We'll be misleading all the people who love you the most. There's a real chance it won't end well."

"It'll be fine." Owen gave her an encouraging smile and opened the driver's door. He came round the vehicle and helped her out as a valet unloaded their bags.

Her eyes widened when he offered her his hand. She slipped hers inside his larger one. This was the first time Owen had made an overt move toward her since their kiss. He was trying to keep his word to stand by her. Maybe they could pull this off after all.

As they approached the doors to the lodge, they opened. Stepping inside, Valerie realized that as glorious as the lodge appeared from the outside, it was more so from the inside. The ceiling soared to a peak with a walkway across the middle and a wide stairway leading to it. At each side of the room were large stone fireplaces high enough for her to stand in. Each had a softly flickering fire. Surrounding them were overstuffed, generously sized leather sofas and chairs that begged her to curl up in them and read. Animal skin rugs adorned the floors. Two large, heavy-looking tables sat in the middle of the room, end to end, separating the two areas.

Off to the side was a bench desk with a young man and woman waiting behind it.

Owen led her in that direction. He spoke to the man. "I'm Owen Clifton. I believe you have a cabin for us."

The man smiled. "Let me have look." He checked his computer screen. "Yes. The Lakeside. You're with the wedding party." He nodded to another young man standing nearby. "Please show Mr. and Mrs. Clifton to the Lakeside cabin."

Valerie felt Owen flinch beside her. She started to correct the title, but decided it was a waste of time.

Soon they were following the man out a side door to where a golf cart waited. Their luggage had already been loaded in the back. Owen helped her into the passenger seat and climbed in beside her. In the tight space his thigh pressed against hers. She couldn't help but be hyperaware of his nearness. When the driver took off, she grabbed the rail on the front seat and Owen's thigh.

Owen's arm came around her shoulders holding her against him. "I'd hate to lose you before the weekend really gets started."

She appreciated the support as well as his touch.

As the golf cart driver motored around sharp turns, she leaned into him. To her astonishment Owen acted pleased to have her pressed against him. Soon they rode over a small bridge with a swiftly flowing brook beneath it. They made another turn that went up a short trail to a rustic-looking cabin with a porch along the front.

Valerie loved it immediately.

The young man pulled the golf cart to a rocking halt. Owen's hold tightened briefly as he said, "Mr. Toad's Wild Ride."

Valerie giggled.

Owen stepped off the cart then helped her down. They started toward the stairs leading to the cabin's porch while the young man unloaded their smaller bags.

On the porch she went to stand beside the railing. The view took her breath away. She inhaled deeply. It was like being in a treehouse with the world spread out below her. The foliage surrounded them and a glade beyond had another brook flowing through it. She couldn't imagine anything more beautiful.

Owen came to stand beside her.

"I love it. I may never leave."

He chuckled. "Let's go inside and see what we have."

In front of the door the man said, "I'll show you inside then finish getting your luggage." He turned the doorknob and opened the door wide.

Owen let her enter first. She walked to the middle of the room. A stone fireplace dominated one side, with a plush looking sofa in front of it. Two armchairs sat at each side. On the shiny wooden floor lay a bright braided rug. The area screamed cozy and romantic. She wasn't sure she had prepared for either of those things. Directly opposite the living area on the other side of the room stood a large bed. Off the bedroom area she noticed a door she assumed went to a bath. In the back corner of the space was a kitchenette, which included a tiny refrigerator.

Just one bed. She would just deal with that.

The walls were decorated with pictures of animals. She guessed they had been painted by local artists. They added to the warm feeling of the space. "This is just perfect."

"I'm glad you like it."

Owen sounded distracted, but she didn't have a chance to ask him more before the young man returned with their second load of luggage.

The man put the luggage near the bed. "When you're ready to come to the lodge just give the desk a call. Someone will come get you. Of course, you're free to walk."

"Thank you." Owen handed the driver a few bills.

When the young man was beyond hearing distance, Owen said, "After that ride I think walking would be safer if he's driving."

Valerie laughed. "It was a rather interesting one." Especially the way she felt pressed against Owen. Her body still tingled at the memory.

He started toward the kitchenette. "I'll let you get settled in. We were supposed to have two bedrooms. I'll call the front desk and see if they have something we can use. Or if you don't mind I'll just take the sofa. Then I don't have to worry about explaining to the kids."

She studied his stature then looked at the sofa and back again before turning her attention to the large bed. "I don't think you'd be very comfortable on it. You're longer than the sofa by at least a foot. I think we can manage in this large bed."

Owen's eyes narrowed. "I don't know."

"Just think about it. I'll stay on my side, and you can stay on yours. It shouldn't be that hard."

"I'll think about it." His tone implied he'd already made up his mind.

Valerie went to unpack, leaving Owen to figure out what he wanted.

A knock on the door brought them both to attention. Before either one of them could answer, a woman's voice called, "Daddy, it's Kaitlyn."

Seconds later a pretty, willowy woman entered, rushing to Owen and giving him a hug. The love was obvious between them. What would it be like to be wrapped in that emotion? Outside of her family Valerie wasn't sure she'd ever known it. She sure hadn't from her ex despite his constant words of love. What he had felt had everything to do with selfishness.

"Is she here?" Kaitlyn stage-whispered.

Valerie stepped from beside the dresser into view. "Are you referring to me?"

Kaitlyn had the good grace to turn red. "John said you were pretty."

Valerie nodded. "Thank you. You must be Kaitlyn. Your father has told me a lot about you."

The younger woman looked from Owen to Valerie and back again. "Dad surprised me when he said you were his date for the weekend."

"Kaitlyn." Owen used a warning tone. His eyes narrowed at his daughter.

"I'm sorry if I've been rude. What I meant was, up until a few weeks ago we didn't know he was dating you, Dr. Hughes."

"Please call me Valerie." She walked into

the kitchenette. "Can I interest you in a cup of tea, Kaitlyn?"

Before she could answer another knock on the door drew their attention. Owen laughed. "That must be the reinforcements." Going to the door, he opened it. "Come in Rich and John. Kaitlyn is already here. This has certainly been a grand welcome."

Valerie smiled. She could appreciate his sarcasm.

"I'm glad you're here. I can make the introduction once." Owen pushed the door wide before coming to stand beside her.

His sons entered.

This would be the true test of how well her and Owen's "relationship" story held up. Valerie feared little made it past the scrutiny of Owen's daughter. They studied each other. She undoubtedly was the image of her mother, who had been a very beautiful woman. And by all standards a saint now.

Owen cleared his throat and put his hand lightly at Valerie's waist, which did nothing to calm her nerves. To the group of three, Owen said, "I've got someone I'd like you to meet." His fingers tightened briefly on her back.

That earned him a point with her. He intended to stand up for her.

John jumped out and said, "I've already met Valerie. She's really nice."

Valerie couldn't imagine how many nice things he would've learned about her from just a short meeting, but it reassured her to hear him. She could appreciate his support.

"Valerie, you've already met my daughter, Kaitlyn. You know John and this is Rich." Owen indicated him with a hand.

"Hi, Rich. It's nice to meet you all. Your father speaks highly of all of you." She made brief eye contact with each of them. Her smile brightened for John.

Rich smiled.

Kaitlyn continued to study Valerie. "We look forward to getting to know you."

"I'm sure with you all being in the wedding party it won't leave you that much time to hang out with us." Owen's hand pressed against Valerie back.

Kaitlyn watched Valerie closely. Owen's daughter might say she wanted him to date but clearly Kaitlyn wanted to pick that person out. Valerie smiled brighter. "Owen, you have a handsome family."

He pressed her against him. "Thank you. I wish I could say their manners were better."

She gave him a light slap on the chest. "Maybe if you talked about me a little more then they wouldn't be so curious." She looked at the children. "Being part of the wedding party sounds like fun."

"Yeah, it should be a good weekend," Kaitlyn said offhandedly. "I brought you a copy of the schedule." She handed it to Owen. "I fixed it so we could all sit at the same table tonight at dinner."

Valerie felt Owen tense as she did. This was definitely becoming overwhelming. She stayed glued to Owen's side. Not a single one of his children missed her action.

Owen spoke up. "That sounds good but for right now I think Valerie and I need to unpack and take a few moments to acclimate ourselves to the place and look over the schedule. We can see each other later this evening."

Kaitlyn hesitated a moment. Rich took his sister's arm and gave her a tug toward the door. "They're waiting on us at the lodge. Aunt Sarah has some kind of get to know each other wedding party mixer planned."

Kaitlyn shook off his hand. "I can take a hint." She glanced back at Valerie and Owen. "I guess we'll see y'all later."

Rich gave Valerie a genuine smile as he followed Kaitlyn out the door with John behind him.

Valerie released a breath she hadn't realized

she'd been holding. "I'm glad you were here when they stopped by."

Owen's smile had turned resigned. "I'm glad I was too. I'm afraid I may owe you big time for helping me when this weekend is over."

She smiled. "What're friends for?"

"I'll let you finish your unpacking in peace." Owen sank into a chair. He hadn't expected to feel so defensive on Valerie's behalf. The need to protect her from his lies to his children made him tense.

He thought he and Valerie would have time to settle in and get used to being in such close quarters before they were invaded by his children. He should have known Kaitlyn would be watching for their arrival.

"I had no idea it would be like this," he said loud enough for Valerie to hear him from the bathroom. "I apologize for the surprise attack. I knew Kaitlyn could be protective, but I didn't expect her to be quite so much so."

"Hey, it's nothing to worry about. I'm good. She just loves her daddy and there's nothing wrong with that."

"I had no idea they'd barge in on us so soon." Apparently, he'd underestimated the situation.

"You had no way of knowing. Why don't I fix us some coffee or tea and we go outside on the porch. We can read the schedule and see what we need to plan for."

"I'll get the drinks. You go on out. Catch your breath for a minute."

A few minutes later Owen carried two mugs of steaming liquid outside. He handed one to Valerie, who sat in a chair.

He took the end of the settee closest to her. "It seems there's a dinner tonight for everyone in my family. It's a barbecue so it's casual dress. Then tomorrow there's golfing for the guys and looks like a spa day for the women. I want you to do that if you wish. You deserve a day of pampering after I got you into this mess."

"Quit worrying about me. Let's concentrate on enjoying the weekend. This is too beautiful of a place to spend our time doing anything but enjoying it." Valerie looked toward the glade.

She really was an attractive woman. The breeze ruffled her hair, and she pushed it back into place. "We do need to take a few minutes to get our stories straight. I promise Kaitlyn will compare hers to what we tell Sarah or Will."

"Let's just tell them the truth. We started seeing each other about three weeks ago. That we've had dinner a few times. That we've known each other for years."

Owen's eyes narrowed in doubt. "Do you think that's going to satisfy Kaitlyn?"

"It'll have to because it's the truth."

He shook his head. "I'm not sure anything is going to satisfy Kaitlyn. She wanted me to find someone, but she sure doesn't seem pleased I found someone."

Valerie made a noise in her throat. "She wants her father happy but doesn't want him to forget her mother. It's only natural."

"Don't let her constantly badger you." The last thing Valerie deserved was that.

"I won't."

Valerie sounded more confident about that happening than he felt. "I'll have a talk with her just to make sure."

Valerie placed her hand on his arm. "Please don't. She just loves you and wants you to be happy."

"I get that, but it doesn't give her the right to interrogate you. Or to make my life miserable either."

She cupped his cheek. "You're sweet. Don't worry about me. I can take care of myself. We haven't really talked about your brother and his wife. Why don't you tell me about them."

"They are the best. I don't know what I would have done without them after Elaine died."

His breath caught. That's the first time he said those words. *Elaine died.* She had passed. She was gone. She left us. But never the reality. The hard fact.

He swallowed the lump in his throat and continued, "Sarah held the house together while Will, my brother, held me together. I think you'll like them. But keep in mind Sarah will be acting crazy this weekend with the wedding and all."

Two hours later, after they'd changed into sweaters and jeans, Owen took Valerie's hand as they walked across the back lawn of the lodge toward an awning containing the wedding party. Music hung in the air while people laughed.

Hoping to calm his and Valerie's nerves, he leaned down to her. "You look lovely tonight."

"Thank you. You don't look half bad yourself."

She'd dressed while he stayed out on the porch. There was something too intimate, too real, too special about sharing a small bathroom with Valerie. He hadn't done anything so personal with a woman in a long time.

When he did go inside, she didn't act the least bit concerned about him being there. Maybe it was because they'd known each other so long. His problem stemmed from him noticing her as more than a friend. Now all he could think about was sliding an arm around her waist, pulling her close and repeating their kiss. Only making it last longer.

She had awakened his body, and his mind hadn't caught up. His heart remained even further behind. Not that he would let that get involved again. Elaine had taken it with her.

"Are you ready for this?" He looked over at the tent.

Valerie's chin rose. "I am. I look forward to meeting all your family."

"You're brave, I'll give you that." He pulled her hand through his arm.

She gave him a tight smile. "I appreciate your support."

For some reason it bothered him that she was only drawing close to look the part of his woman friend for the others. He would have liked it if being near him mattered to her.

As they stepped under the canopy, a tall, dark-haired man who looked like Owen stopped talking to a group and hurried toward them with a smile on his face. "Owen. It's great to see you." They hugged each other, with back slaps.

Owen pulled away to draw Valerie close. "Valerie, I'd like you to meet my brother, Will."

Will smiled warmly at Valerie. "I'm so glad you could join us. Really glad."

Owen's heart hurt for the worry he had caused his brother.

Sarah rushed over to join them. She treated Valerie just as warmly. It pricked Owen's conscious for a moment that he wasn't being truthful with them. He'd come clean when given a chance.

Sarah pulled on Will's arm. "We have to go. It's almost time for our welcome." She looked at Owen and Valerie and waved toward the long buffet table. "Go help yourself. We'll see you later."

They were halfway down the table when Owen heard Rich's voice behind him. "Hey, Dad, we're at that table at the back." He pointed. "We saved y'all seats."

"Okay." With Rich gone Owen brushed Valerie ear with his lips. "Are you ready for this?"

She smiled. "As I'll ever be."

Owen couldn't help but be proud of Valerie's attitude.

* * *

A few minutes later with their plates full, he and Valerie joined his children. He wasn't surprised to learn that Kaitlyn had arranged the seating so she would be next to Valerie.

Valerie had thought it through while dressing. The best defense was an offense. Now was the time to see how it worked. She smiled at everyone at the table as she slid into the seat next to Kaitlyn. Giving the younger woman her attention Valerie looked past her to the thin young man sitting on her right. "Your daddy tells me you're married. This must be your husband."

Kaitlyn's eyes widened. "Yes, this is Robert."

"It's nice to meet you, Robert." Valerie offered him a smile.

He returned a shy one. "It's nice to meet you as well."

Valerie settled her napkin in her lap and looked at her plate. "Wow, this looks great."

Before she took the first bite she said to Kaitlyn, "Y'all are staying in the lodge. How're the rooms?"

Kaitlyn took the bait and started describing in detail their room. Valerie listened patiently and continue to ask more questions when Kaitlyn paused.

Owen pressed his thigh against hers, making heat run along her leg. She glanced at him. He grinned. Valerie looked at Rich. "I understand you're thinking about being doctor like your dad. He's a really fine one."

Rich told her about his struggle to decide what direction he wanted his life to take.

Owen shifted and lay his arm across the back of Valerie's chair. The tips of his fingers caressed her shoulder. Once again, the action did not go unnoticed by his children. He played his part well. "I think it's time y'all give Valerie a break and let her finish her meal."

A woman Valerie didn't recognize stood behind the microphone in front of the group. "I need all of the wedding party up here."

Owen's children shuffled out of their chairs.

Valerie commented to no one in particular left at the table. "I could use some dessert."

Kaitlyn's husband volunteer to go after it.

As he left Owen chuckled. "I had no idea you were such a great actress."

It was nice to know she could surprise Owen and had his gratitude. She twisted her mouth into a funny little grin. "Maybe I wasn't acting." Now she was flirting.

Owen's gaze met hers and held it.

Will approached them, interrupting the moment. "Owen, I have you down to play golf in my foursome tomorrow morning, but one of the guys has dropped out. We need to find someone to fill his spot. Do you think one of your boys would be willing?"

"I never could get Rich or John interested." Owen shook his head. "I'm not much help."

Will's lips formed a tight line. "If I don't find someone to fill the spot, we'll have to forfeit. I hate to do that. I have a little money on the game with the father-in-law to be."

"Could I help?" Valerie offered.

"Have you played any golf?" Owen asked.

"Some."

Will thumped the back of her chair. "Then you're in. A warm body is better than no body. I'll see you both at the club house in the morning. We have an eight thirty tee off." He hurried away with a smile on his face.

"I didn't know you played golf." Owen looked at her with curiosity. "You've never said anything."

"I've never had a reason to do so. The subject has never come up."

Robert returned with her dessert. She took a bite. A perfect apple pie.

Owen watched her eat. She had a way of moving her lips across a fork that made his middle quiver. "Are you sure you want to spend the day on the golf course instead of at the spa?"

"I think some spa time would be great after a round of golf. Maybe you could join me."

"What?" He shook his head as he sat back in the chair.

She grinned at the squeak in Owen's voice. "You don't like spas?"

"I wouldn't know."

Her look dared him. "You should try it. There's nothing like a good massage."

"Maybe I will." What had gotten into him? He'd never thought of going to a spa before in his life. "Why don't we call it a night? I think we've both had about all we want for one day, and apparently, we'll have a full one tomorrow. That restful weekend I promised you is slowly turning into a lie."

She could not argue with that. He stood and pulled her chair out. Owen was a gentleman and she liked that.

"Do you want to take the golf cart back or walk?" He led her out from under the tent.

Valerie looked at the star-studded sky. "I think I'd enjoy a walk. It's a beautiful night."

He took her hand as they started across the lawn. It reassured her to have her hand in his. She had started to like too many things about Owen. Even when they moved along the lit path to the cabin, he continued to hold her hand. They walked in silence. A little breeze ruffled the dried leaves at their feet and caused others to fall around them. Somehow the quietness wasn't uncomfortable, instead peaceful.

It wasn't until they reacted the cabin that Valerie remembered they would be spending the night in small space—together. Had it crossed Owen's mind as well? They were both adults so they could handle the situation. She had no doubt Owen would be considerate and would never apply pressure to do anything she didn't want to. The puzzling bit was that she now wanted more than she should.

Owen followed her up to the porch. She waited as he unlocked the door then allowed her to go in first. They stood in the living area for a moment as if unsure about what to do next.

He cleared his throat. "It's a little cool in here. I think I'll turn on the fire."

"I'm going to have a cup of tea. Would you like one? Or coffee?" She needed to do something to keep busy.

"Tea is fine."

Soon the gas logs were glowing.

Valerie's hands shook slightly as she made the tea. She could have been on her first date as nervous as she acted around him. What was happening between them? Despite having a crush on him for years, she'd never felt the sexual attraction she did this evening. It stimulated her and scared her at the same time. The right thing to do would be not to act on it.

She carried the steaming mugs over to where Owen sat in one of the two chairs. He had pulled them closer to the fire. His shoes were set on the floor while his bare feet were on the hearth and crossed at the ankles. She'd never seen him more relaxed. A direct contradiction to her rattled nerves.

Valerie handed him a mug and then eased down into the other chair while holding hers. She took a sip of the hot liquid, letting it heat her from the inside out.

"Mmm…" rolled from Owen's lips. "I'm not normally a tea drinker, but this is really good. It hits the spot tonight." He set his mug down on the table nearby before he laid his head against the back of the chair and close his eyes.

Valerie watched him. Owen had aged well and probably would continue to do so. No wonder all the nurses, young and old, had a crush on him. She couldn't help but be a member of his fan club too.

"Valerie, tell me why you're not married or

don't have someone special in your life. The truth if you don't mind. It won't go any further than me. Promise."

Her heart jerked. Could she share that ugly story? She looked at him, but his eyes were still closed. "How do you know I don't?"

"Because you're here with me. You would never be disloyal, and if you belonged to me, I'd never let you go off and do something like this with another man. Even if you were just friends."

If he only knew.

"The more I'm around you the more amazing I find you. You were a real champ tonight. I just don't understand why you don't have anybody special."

Glad his eyes remained closed she said, "It's not because I haven't had the chance."

Owen rolled his head to the side and opened one eye. "What happened?"

"He decided he wanted his wife more." She didn't try to hide the bitterness.

His eyes opened wide, and he sat up. "What?"

"Yes, I had an affair with a married man. Only I didn't know he was married." She would get it all out and be done with it. Owen could send her home if he wished. "You asked me why I moved to Atlanta. He was why. He was a visiting doctor and swept me off my feet. Only thing is, he never wanted to be seen with me. Sometimes he would disappear for the weekend and not say where he'd been. One day I heard some of the nurses talking about seeing him, his wife and their kids at the zoo. I couldn't get to the bathroom fast enough to throw up. When I said I would no longer have anything to do with him, he retaliated by making sure everyone knew I had been sleeping with him. I had to start looking for a job elsewhere. Now you know my dirty big secret."

Owen shook his head. His hands fisted on the arms of the chair. "He was a... I can't think of a word strong enough to describe him."

"I can't disagree." Her attention went to the fire.

"Now I understand why you reacted the way you did when I was a jerk. It reminded you too much of him. I'm sorry."

She closed her eyes and open them again. "You didn't know. I haven't exactly had a great track record with men. I tend to be left behind. Even my father left when I was five."

"That must've been very difficult."

"My mom and siblings, we worked through it. After I got through school, I just focused on my job. It was one place where I felt security. The men in my life haven't exactly proved worthy of my admiration. Present company excluded."

"Thanks. I sure hope I'm not lumped into your usual group of men. I will endeavor to be better than that."

She stood. "I'm sure you are already." If anything, he was loyal. He proved that by how he clung to his dead wife. "I'm going to get ready for bed unless you want the bathroom first."

"No, you can have it."

A few minutes later, when she exited the bath, she found Owen stretched out on the sofa with a pillow under his head and a blanket pulled over him. She quietly slipped into bed and turned off the light.

"Good night, Valerie. I'm glad you came with me."

Warmth like a furry blanket on a freezing day went through her. "You're welcome."

CHAPTER SIX

OWEN WOKE TO the smell of coffee. It had been a long time since that had been the case. He stretched. Looking over the end of the couch, he saw Valerie moving around the kitchenette.

How could any man have treated Valerie with such callous disregard? She was a wonderful woman who didn't deserve the kind of treatment she received in her life. Any man in his right mind would want her. To make matters worse, he'd acted as if he were ashamed of her more than once. No wondered she looked at him as if he had kicked her. If he were available, he would make her feel as appreciated as she deserved.

Dressed for the day in a pullover sweater and tan slacks, Valerie had tucked her hair under a ballcap. She looked both very appealing and ready for the golf course. "Good morning." His voice came out as a gravelly whisper. He cleared his throat. "Mornin'."

Valerie turned. "Hey, sleepyhead. How about a cup of coffee?"

"Sounds wonderful."

She brought a mug to him.

"Coffee in bed. I could get use to this." There was a number of things about Valerie he could get used to. A tint of color came to her cheeks. It was refreshing to see someone her age could still blush. It made him feel rather manly to have her respond that way. "I see you're ready for the day."

"I am. You better get moving. I've let you sleep as long as I could. We won't make our tee time if you don't hurry." She returned to the kitchenette.

He raised the mug. "Let me get this coffee down and I'll be ready to go in just a few minutes."

"I found some muffins in the cabinet with a note that they are for us." She pulled a couple of plates from a shelf.

"Great. I'm starving." He pushed the covers back as he placed his feet on the floor.

Valerie's stare made him wonder what was wrong. He'd forgotten he only wore his boxers. He watched her studying him. She flattered him with her interest.

After a few moments she said, "I'll get out of your way and finish up in the bathroom."

Owen grinned. She was so bold in some ways then timid in others. He found the combination intriguing.

He finished his coffee and had a muffin before he strolled into the bedroom area. Valerie brushed passed him on her way into the living room. Yes, this was fine morning entertainment. He missed moments like this. Sharing a space with someone.

Forty-five minutes later they were outside the clubhouse ready to start their game. Owen had rented Valerie a set of clubs and golf shoes. He had been surprised at the time and attention she had given to picking both out.

Will introduced him and Valerie to the father of the bride, who was heading up the foursome they were playing against. The other man in their foursome was Sarah's brother.

Promptly at eight thirty the men teed off. Owen was pleased with his drive.

"Do you want to drive the cart or shall I?" he asked Valerie when it was time to move up to the women's tee.

"You're welcome to do it." Did she suspected he was one of those guys who'd rather drive than be driven?

Owen stopped beside the women's tee. Valerie found her driver club and took her stance, ready to swing. He had enjoyed too much the movement of her hips as she warmed up. He had to get his mind back where it belonged. Nothing in their agreement said anything about him ogling Valerie.

With a beautiful swing, she contacted with the ball and sent it flying. It landed not far from his in the fairway. He whispered in admiration, "Nice shot."

The other men agreed.

After she returned to the cart, Owen gave her a narrow-eyed look. "You've been sand-bagging me. Last night you implied you haven't played much, but I don't think that's true."

Her look turned sheepish, and she wouldn't meet his gaze. "I haven't played much lately. At least not in the last few years."

"But you have played a lot at one time."

"I had a golfing scholarship for college. We won nationals two years in a row." She squinched up her face. "I had the best handicap."

He chuckled. "I should have known. I shouldn't be surprised, but I am. You've never said anything about enjoying golf. Obviously there're some mysteries about you."

She winked. "If you hang around more, you just might learn what they are."

Owen laughed. He might like that. "We'll

start with planning to play a round or two of golf on our next day off."

"Sounds like a plan. Now let's finish this one."

They continued to play the hole. On the second shot, Valerie and he both made the edge of the green. With chip shots they were in a good position to the hole. He made the cup in two putts and her in one.

"You were amazing. Excellent playing."

"I'm glad you like it. I'm a little rusty." She went pink with pride and pleasure at his approval.

"I'd hate to play against you if you weren't rusty."

Her eyes twinkled. "I'd hate it for you too."

Hours later their foursome returned to the clubhouse as the victors.

"You were wonderful." Owen gave Valerie a hug. She returned it. It continued longer than necessary, but she liked being surrounded by Owen.

Will joined them, making them break apart. "We had a ringer, and we didn't even know it. I was glad to have you. I needed this win. Gives me bragging rights."

Valerie smiled as she finished cleaning her clubs. "I'm glad I could help."

Owen took her bag from her. "Now it's time

you do something for yourself. I'm sending you to the spa for the afternoon."

"Right now, I'd rather have some food." She looked toward the lodge.

Owen nodded. "Food first, then the spa."

They returned her clubs and shoes and stored his equipment to be picked up later before they strolled to the lodge.

"I had a good time this morning." Valerie lifted her face to the sun.

Owen took her hand. "I did too."

As they sat at a table near a window, Valerie picked up one half of her club sandwich.

"What's on the schedule for this afternoon?"

"As far as I know, for us nothing. Free time." Owen bit into his hamburger. "While you're at the spa I'll just go back to the cabin."

"You could come to the spa with me." She looked at him with half-lidded eyes.

He shook his head. "I think I'll just go watch some TV. Maybe check in with the kids. I'm not much of a spa person."

"You can't knock it until you've tried it. I think you might be surprised how much you like it. Think steam room, hot tub, massage, facial, pedicure, manicure—"

Owen held up a hand. "No facial, pedicure,

or manicure for me. But I have to admit a good steam room sounds nice."

She laughed. "But I want you to get a massage as well. I promise you'll like it. As far as I'm concerned, you haven't lived until you've had one. So what do you say?"

He said nothing for a few moments. "Okay, I'll go along. This time."

Two hours later, Valerie lay on her stomach with her face pillowed through a hole in the masseuse's table. Wrapped in nothing but a towel, Owen lay next to her in the same position.

She grinned every time she heard a moan or a groan from him.

Soft music played in the room. She had been shocked when he had suggested a couple's massage. Apparently he hadn't realized they would be undressed in a room together. For him to do something so private surprised her. He'd spent the last few weeks keeping her at arm's length. Yet she had to admit he had loosened up. She questioned his judgment, but he insisted it was the way he wanted it. He had even accused her of being insecure.

"Oh, that feels good. That's the spot," Owen softly muttered.

Did he make that type of noise when making love? Her body stiffened and heated.

"Are you okay ma'am?"

"I'm fine." As long as she didn't think about Owen lying naked only a feet away.

"You're done sir," Owen's masseuse said. "Just lie here and take it easy for as long as you wish. Be careful when standing and be sure to drink a lot of water."

Owen released a slow sigh.

A few minutes later her masseuse said the same to her as Owen's had and slipped out the door. She and Owen were left wearing nothing but a towel. The lights remained dim with soft music playing.

Valerie's nerves prickled. She hadn't counted on this situation. And she'd thought staying in the cabin was close quarters. Hearing nothing from Owen for a few minutes, she wondered if he was sleeping or just pretending.

Finally, the soft sound of his voice surrounded her. "I'm glad you made me do this."

"I didn't know I made you."

"I wasn't a willing partner." He shifted on the table.

"That I'll agree with." She turned her head to look at him.

His gaze met hers. "But I have to say I'd be

willing to do it again. I now understand why people want to go to the spa."

"I'm glad you enjoyed yourself." His look heated her body.

"I've really been having a good time with you. I'm glad I asked you to come along. This weekend would've been much harder without you."

Her feminine parts had begun to tingle. "I've had a good time as well. I guess if we're going to make it to the rehearsal dinner tonight we'd better get moving. Even though I hate the thought of getting up."

"Me too."

She wanted him out of the room for when she crawled off the table. The chance of losing her towel was too great. "Why don't you go first, then I'll meet you outside the dressing room." She didn't shy away from watching him roll from the table. The view was too tempting.

Thinking he had left, she tried shifting off the table, but her muscles didn't want to cooperate. She groaned.

"Hey, are you okay? Do I need to help you?"

Valerie jerked to a stop. Owen stood beside her. Securing the towel around her, she rolled over hoping the towel didn't flap open. She wiggled from the table, but her muscles were so weak her knees buckled.

Owen moved quickly, steadying her. "Let me help you."

Valerie looked at him. His eyes were on her lips. Her skin burned where his hands touched. Her breathing was ragged. He was going to kiss her. She wanted this. Craved it. She gripped his forearms. His lips had just found hers when there was a knock at the door.

She jerked back, her towel catching on the table corner and tugging it loose from where it had been tucked in at her breasts. "Oh." Valerie grab for the material but it went to the floor.

The knock came again.

"We'll be right out," Owen answered, eyes never leaving her body. He reached for her towel and handed it to her. "You'll want to cover up, I'm sure. Do you need help?"

With a heated face, she snatched the towel from him and quickly wrapped it around herself. She walked out the door with her head held high. Moments later with robes on, they walked toward the locker room.

As they were entering the room, Kaitlyn and Robert stepped out dressed in robes. The entire group stopped short, in shock.

"Hey, Daddy."

"Hi, honey. I hope you've been having a good day." Owen acted as if it were no big deal for them all to stand there in almost no clothing.

"We have. What have you two been up too?" Kaitlyn looked from one to the other of them.

Valerie feared she might be hot enough to combust.

Owen took Valerie's hand. "We played golf this morning and just got out of the most amazing couple's massage." He squeezed her hand. Was he teasing his daughter?

Kaitlyn's look focused on their clasped hands. "I didn't know you got massages."

"There's a lot of things you probably don't know about me, honey."

Kaitlyn gave Valerie a perplexed look. "I'm glad to know you're having a good time."

Owen pulled Valerie close to his side. "We're having a great time. We're off to get ready for the rehearsal dinner. See you there."

Kaitlyn didn't look overjoyed with idea. "Okay."

With the door to the locker room between them, Valerie looked at Owen with a grin. He returned it and they broke into laugher.

Owen kissed her temple. "She wanted me

to have someone to do things with. Now she's gotten her wish, but I'm not so sure she's happy about it."

An hour and a half later Owen dressed in his navy blue suit in the living area, listening to Valerie getting ready for the evening. He kept his eyes squarely on the football game playing on TV. Yet he had no idea what the name of the teams were nor the score.

He couldn't believe it. He'd almost kissed her. Again. Then when her towel had dropped away, his breath had left him. He hadn't wanted a woman since Elaine died. Before that he'd been in college. Despite their friendship, all he could think about was touching and holding Valerie. There was nothing friendly about his feelings. He'd planned a simple weekend that had spiraled completely out of control emotionally. The need to have her had become almost a living thing. Too old for this kind of nonsense, he had to control his actions. And reactions.

"I'm ready if you are," Valerie said in a cheery voice.

He turned to find her standing there wearing a deep royal blue dress that wrapped her waist and tied at one hip. It complemented her coloring perfectly. Small diamonds twinkled in her ears. A necklace that matched the diamonds hung around her long neck. A gleam of confidence filled her eyes.

Wow. "What's the plan? To outdo the bride?"

That made her eyes sparkle brighter. A smile appeared on her pink-covered lips. "You sure know how to make a woman feel good. Thank you."

"Hey, I'm the one feeling good. All the other men are going to be envious you are with me." So many times he had seen her in scrubs with a surgical cap on her head. He'd glimpsed her curves, but tonight Valerie was all woman. She would be his woman, on his arm. He would be proud to say she was with him.

Until the end of the weekend. Would he be ready for them to go back to just friendship? He couldn't say that he would.

Her smile grew. "I had no idea you were such a silver tongued devil."

"I, too, have some surprises left in me." He offered his arm.

She wrapped hers through it. "I look forward to finding out what they are."

Was Valerie flirting with him? He liked the idea. "I called for a golf cart. I didn't think you'd want to walk down there in your high heels."

"That's thoughtful of you."

He stayed close as she made her way down the steps. He didn't want her to fall. The protection of Valerie was a new emotion for him. He'd never been that way with Elaine.

The golf cart arrived just as they made it down the stairs. Soon they were pulling up to the lodge.

The night's festivities had been planned in a large, elegant room off the lobby. The space consisted of an open area with a high ceiling and walls of windows. Round tables laid with crisp, snow-white tablecloths and sparkling silverware filled the room.

As they entered, Will buzzed by them long enough to say that Owen and Valerie would be sitting at his and Sarah's table that evening. Will pointed in the direction of the front left. Soon they found Sarah holding court at the table. Searching the place markers, they found their seats.

His children were seated at the next table. Valerie stood beside him as he greeted each one of them.

"Hey, Dad. Tell us about having a massage. I didn't know you went in for those sorts of things." Rich's voice held a large dose of teasing. The grin on his face confirmed it. Kaitlyn had no doubt been on the phone with her brothers before he and Valerie left the spa.

"As a doctor I highly recommend one." Especially the kiss afterward. But he wouldn't say that.

He glanced at Valerie. She had a shy grin on her lips. She acted as if she enjoyed him being put on the spot.

"I've never known you to go for a massage." John looked perplexed by who his father had become.

"I haven't. But I have to admit the experience was quite invigorating." He winked at Valerie whose cheeks pinkened. "I look forward to doing it again."

"I didn't take you as the kind of person who would go for a couple's massage." Kaitlyn watched him and Valerie closely.

Owen shrugged. "You know, you never should get too old to try new things."

Kaitlyn's jaw dropped.

He looked at each one of his children. "Isn't that what you guys told me just a few weeks ago?"

"Yeah, but—"

A woman behind the microphone cut off the rest of Kaitlyn's sentence.

"I can tell you all about it later." Owen heard Valerie's soft giggle. He smiled at her as he helped her into her chair.

"You're being mean to them," she whispered.

"They deserve it. They have been messing in my business."

She hissed, "They're going to think I'm some floozie who's corrupting their father."

He found her hand, lifted it to his lips, then kissed the back of it. "Aren't you?"

She leaned closer. He picked up a hint of something floral on her skin. He wanted to tug her nearer but dare not. "I think you're starting to enjoy this tall tale we've created. Especially the shock value for your children."

"I can't say that I'm not." All of it. Especially touching her. "That's a cherry on top of my weekend."

Valerie's eyes looked worried. Her lips thinned. "I just hope it doesn't backfire on both of us."

Over the next hour and a half, they enjoyed the conversation with those at their table. Valerie fit in perfectly. He couldn't have made a better choice about who to ask to the wedding. If it hadn't been Valerie, he didn't know who he would have asked. It didn't matter because she had come, and she was great. Almost too great. One day he would have to own up to his family what he had done.

When it became time for the speeches, he

couldn't resist reaching for Valerie's hand. She accepted it. He held it, not caring if anyone saw them. At one point he leaned in close to her ear. "I'm sorry to put you through this."

"I don't mind. I'm enjoying the chance to get to know your family."

"I'm not sure it's the way I want you to know them."

The speeches dragged on. The event wouldn't be over soon enough for him. He looked forward to spending some time alone with Valerie. He planned to finish that kiss he started.

By the time they were leaving, thunder rumbled off in the distance. They made a mad dash for the closest empty golf cart. It had started sprinkling by the time they got to their cabin. They hurried up the steps, just making the porch before the downpour begun.

Valerie moved toward the settee. "I love to listen to the rain. I think I'll sit out here for a few minutes."

"Do you mind if I join you?"

"No at all. That would be nice." She patted the cushion next to her.

"Would you like a cup of tea to go with the rain?"

"That would be wonderful. I'll go fix it." She moved to get up.

He waved her down. "I'll get it."

Owen hurried to the kitchenette and started the water for tea. While it heated, he turned on the fire so the room would be warm when they came in. Pulling a throw off the back of the couch, he stepped out long enough to hand it to Valerie.

"Thank you."

He soon returned with two steaming mugs in hand and joined her on the settee. He liked that he could feel her heat all the way up one side of his body.

She wrapped her hands around the mug. "This is great. I'm glad you thought about it."

"Warm enough?"

"Yes. You have taken good care of me. The blanket is keeping me warm and the tea hits the spot."

They were quiet for a few minutes, just enjoying the peace of the rain.

"You have a very nice family. I hope they won't be too mad when you tell them we are just pretending." She took a sip of tea.

"They'll get over it. My family loves me. They won't kick me out."

"That's nice to know. Not everyone has that type of security. Your nephew seems to be marrying into a very nice family." She took another sip of tea.

"He is." Owen put his mug down on the floor of the porch.

They returned to listening to the rain as it drummed against the tin of the roof. After a few minutes Owen turned to Valerie, taking her mug and setting it beside his.

She gave him a quizzical look.

"I'd like to finish what I started in the massage room. Let me know if you have a problem with that." With no objection on Valerie's part his lips found hers.

There was nothing tentative about the meeting of their mouths. This time Valerie wrapped her arms around his neck. She leaned into him. He accepted her assent while requesting she opened her mouth. He entered and found heaven.

His hands tightened on her, bringing her securely to him as he deepened the kiss. Pure moments of bliss followed. Owen wanted more. This and so much more he'd been missing in his life.

Placing a hand on his chest, Valerie pulled back. "Are you sure this is what you want? Just a couple of weeks ago you ran away. Headed for the hills anytime somebody even saw us together. I can't take being pushed and pulled. I'd rather not to begin with."

He couldn't help but hang his head in

shame. "I know I've been slow to get used to it. Elaine and I had been together for a lot of years. It's hard for me to think about kissing, touching or have anything to do with another woman."

"Yet here you're kissing me."

"Yeah, I couldn't be more surprised." He looked at the crack in the wood floor.

"I'm not sure whether to be flattered or upset about that statement."

He tugged at his collar. "I can assure you it's to be flattered. You're the first woman I've wanted to touch in years."

Valerie smiled. "That I can be flattered about. But I don't want us to take things too fast. Make a step that you're not going to be uncomfortable with or will regret. Especially since we're cooped up together this weekend. It could just be that I'm convenient. I think we need to take it slow and easy."

"I don't know how easy that's going to be. I sure do enjoy your kisses."

Valerie chuckled. "I didn't say it would be easy." She stood. "Come on. Let's go in. I'm getting damp out here."

The rain had become a downpour. He hadn't noticed until that moment. They left the porch and entered the cabin. "Want to sit by the fire for a while?"

"That sounds nice. Let me get out of these clothes, especially the heels. That's one of the best things about being in the OR. I can wear my clogs." She headed for the bedroom area.

Owen shrugged out of his suit jacket then pulled off his shoes. He sat on the sofa, propping his feet up to the warmth of the fire. Valerie returned in PJs. The message was clear. The sign obviously read closed for the night, and he would honor her wishes. She was right; they needed to take it slow. The one thing he didn't want was to ruin their friendship or make it impossible to work together.

Valerie sat down beside him. To his pleasure she scooted close and took his hand. "This is nice." She laid her head against his shoulder.

"I agree."

For a long time, they said nothing as they watched the fire. These were the kind of moments he had missed, wanted again. Just something as simple as the companionship of having another person in the room. Valerie had a way about her that soothed his soul.

Soon her head became heavier against his shoulder and her hand relaxed. She slept.

Slowly scooting away from her, he gently shook her awake. "Valerie, it's time we get you to bed. You fell asleep." She made the sweetest moan, but he remained focused on the issue at hand. "Come on, honey, let me help you to bed." He urged her to stand then led her to the bed. Flipping the covers back, he said, "Let me get this housecoat off you." Beneath he found she wore classic pants pajamas, which did nothing to detract from her sexiness.

She lay on the bed and he pulled the sheet and blanket over her. "A man couldn't ask for a better fake girlfriend than you. I appreciate your friendship. I couldn't ask for a better one." He kissed her on the forehead. He turned off the light and headed back to the sofa.

Her sleepy voice came from behind him. "You're too big for that sofa. Sleep in the bed tonight."

His back and legs would appreciate a wider and longer space. But could he manage to spend the night without touching her? He would give it a try. Removing his clothes, Owen climbed into the bed. A gulf lay between him and Valerie that he intended to maintain until she was ready to build a bridge. It might be difficult, but he would do it.

Rolling on his side away from Valerie, he pretended she wasn't there all warm, sweet smelling and kind. He hoped he could get some rest, yet he'd set himself up for failure.

* * *

Valerie woke huddled against warm skin. Her back pressed against something hard. An arm hung over her waist. Her eyes whipped open. She lay snuggled against Owen. On his side of the bed. Apparently during the night she'd gotten cold and been drawn to his heat.

His breathing ruffled her hair at the shell of her ear. She couldn't deny it felt good being pressed against him. She had been the one to set the boundary, then she'd gone and crossed it. She needed to move or decide on what she wanted their relationship to be. She wasn't prepared to do so yet.

But she wanted to stay. She needed to go. But she was so warm. She had to get up.

She wanted him to recognize she wasn't a substitute for his dead wife or not there just to be a fun time. She really cared for him. More than a friend, but she had to protect her heart, too. She'd been left behind enough, betrayed, and she didn't care for Owen being another man on her list who had left her. She would rather they remain friends.

She shifted.

Owen's arm tightened. "Where are you going? You're nice and warm."

"It's time to get up."

"We have a few more minutes, don't we?"

His voice rumbled near her ear. "This is the way to wake up every morning. I've missed you."

Every muscle in Valerie's body tensed. Owen thought she was Elaine!

Valerie wasted no time moving out from under his arm and across the bed. She got up, not bothering to look at him as she grabbed her clothes. "I'm sorry. I didn't mean to get over on your side."

He rolled to his back. "No problem at all."

She glanced at him, but her look stuck on his bare chest showing above the sheet that had dropped to his waist. "We better get moving."

"What's the hurry? The wedding isn't until this afternoon. We have the day to ourselves."

She headed toward the bath. "You didn't read the schedule. We have a family brunch this morning. They'll want you in the family pictures they're taking afterward."

Owen groaned. "I'd rather stay here cuddled up in bed with you."

"Not an option." She threw the words over her shoulder. That wasn't going to happen. He didn't even recognize the difference between her and his dead wife. That might be the supreme rejection.

He stretched his arms over his head and

flexed. "You go on without me and tell me about it later."

Valerie glared at him. "That's not going to happen. I'm getting dressed. Why don't you start the coffee?"

His brows narrowed. "Are you running away from me?"

"No."

"Seems to me that you're trying to put some space between us."

She turned, walking to the end of the bed to glare down at him. "Just who did you think was in bed with you just a minute ago?"

"Well, you, of course."

"So why did you make it sound like you thought I was Elaine? You said you missed me." He had the good grace to look ashamed. "I'm sorry. I must not have been awake yet. I would never intentionally hurt you."

"I'm not a replacement for your dead wife. Please keep that in mind."

He didn't blink. "I know that."

She continued to glare. "When you're kissing me, are you thinking of her?"

He jerked to a sitting position. "I can assure you I'm thinking of you. Come here. I can prove it."

"I don't know if I can believe you." She marched to the bathroom.

* * *

She had her coffee in hand when Owen entered the kitchen area wearing a T-shirt and jeans. His bare feet padded across the wooden floor.

His bigger body boxed her in. "Hey, I didn't mean to hurt your feelings. I can assure you I know exactly who you are. You're sweet, caring Valerie who I've seen talk to a scared child and have them laughing a few minutes later. You're the doctor who worries over her patient even when they've been discharged. The friend who helps out a friend when he has a crazy idea." He took a step closer. "You're the woman who can beat the socks off most men on a golf course, including me. You're the person who went along with the idea of getting a couple's massage when I suggested it." He walked closer. "You're the woman who has bested Kaitlyn, which I wouldn't have thought possible."

Valerie chuckled.

He cupped her cheek. "You're the woman who has me thinking about nothing but kissing her again." His lips found hers. The kiss was gentle and sincere. She melted against him.

He pulled away. "Am I forgiven? It won't happen again. Promise."

She smiled and nodded.

"Good. We only have one more day in this beautiful place, and I'd like to make the most of it."

"Sounds like a plan. I guess we start by having brunch with your children."

Owen made a face. "I had other ideas but if we must."

Valerie couldn't help but forgive Owen for his faux pas after the sweet speech he gave. Few people saw through her as well as he did. They just had today and tomorrow before they were back to the real world, and she didn't want to spend the time angry. Yet it better not happen again.

The sun shone bright, so they agreed to walk to the lodge for brunch.

She looked at the sky. "It's going to be a beautiful day for a wedding."

"Yeah. I'm not much into weddings. I'm only here for Will and the kids. Otherwise, I could pass on the wedding."

"I had no idea you were such a cynic." She didn't really mind. Lots of people didn't care about weddings.

"And I had no idea you were such a romantic."

She swung their hands between them. "There's nothing wrong with being a romantic."

SUSAN CARLISLE 161

He grinned. "Or being a cynic."

Owen's children were already in the dining room when they arrived. Valerie was determined to win over Kaitlyn. Smiling warmly, Valerie greeted each of them. "Kaitlyn, do you mind if I sit beside you?"

The look of surprise on the woman's face spoke volumes. She hadn't expected that from Valerie. She smiled to herself. Valerie had already gained the upper hand.

"Sure." Kaitlyn moved so Valerie could more easily take her chair.

"Great. We really haven't had a good chance to get to know each other."

"Uh, no, we haven't."

Valerie reached for her napkin. "I'd like to change that."

"Really?" The word was but a squeak.

Owen's soft chuckle beside Valerie spurred her on. He started a conversation with his son-in-law.

Valerie turned to Kaitlyn. "I understand you and Robert live in Marietta. How're you enjoying that?"

"We're happy there. We're starting to look for a house."

"That sounds like fun. I've lived in apartments or condos most of my life. Every once in a while, I think about buying a house."

"Why haven't you done it?" She had Valerie's full attention now.

"I guess I think of a house as being a place for two people. It's just me…"

"You've never been married?"

"No." Valerie just hoped she didn't ask why.

"So, no house?"

"So, no house."

Kaitlyn face turned serious and thoughtful. "Dad lives in the big old house we grew up in."

"It's a lovely home." Valerie looked at her with understanding.

Kaitlyn had a moment of thought. "That's right, you were there the other night when John came home."

"I was. Your dad showed off all your pictures. Including your mom. She was a lovely lady. You look a lot like her."

The pleasure on Kaitlyn's face let Valerie know she'd said the correct thing. Valerie placed her hand over Kaitlyn's. "I know you miss her every day."

"Yeah, I do." Her eyes glistened.

"Your dad does too. I'm glad he has you guys." Valerie looked at her brothers. "It's good to have someone around you who loves you."

"I've been worried about Dad. He's been

pretty resistant to going out. We were all surprised to learn about you."

"You were?" Valerie offered Kaitlyn her best innocent expression, pushing the guilt down about misleading Owen's children.

"Yeah, he didn't say anything to us about dating you. You were a complete surprise when he announced he'd be bringing someone to the wedding."

Valerie glanced at Owen. "Your dad and I have been friends for a long time. We've worked together for a number of years."

"I can remember hearing him mention your name a few times but never as a girlfriend. I'm just surprised because he was so firmly against me trying to fix him up with somebody."

Valerie lowered her voice, keeping it even. "What are you most aggravated about? Is it that your dad's found somebody or that he did it without your help?"

Kaitlyn leaned back with a shocked look as if that had never occurred to her.

"Yeah," John said from the other side of the table, then chuckled. "She's not the one in charge."

Kaitlyn glared at her brother. "I just want Daddy to be happy."

"I think spending time with me makes your

father happy. We enjoy each other's company. Isn't that what you want for him?"

Kaitlyn was slow to answer. "I did. I do. I have to admit he doesn't seem like the same person he was even a few weeks ago."

"That's because you're seeing him in a different light now. He's a person as well as being your father. He has a life outside of what you're used to."

Rich spoke up. "She's got you there, Kaitlyn."

After that Valerie turned her attention to Rich. It turned out they both liked old movies. They got into a debate about which was the best. Soon the topic of conversation for the entire table went to football and what teams were playing that day. It became a family discussion that fascinated Valerie.

At one point Owen reached under the table and squeezed her thigh. She looked at him. His gaze met hers. He mouthed *Thank you*.

With brunch at an end, Valerie and Owen walked the long way back to the cabin while his children went to go get ready for the wedding.

Owen took her hand, holding it securely. "You were great with Kaitlyn. I think you have gotten her off my back about dating."

"Kaitlyn and I came to an understanding.

I still hated to mislead them about our relationship."

"It's a risk I'm willing to take if it'll give me peace."

Later that afternoon Owen was once again dressed in a suit waiting on Valerie. He tugged at his black-and-gray-striped tie that looked best with his black suit. The afternoon had turned cool. He waited by the fireplace, warming his hands.

When Valerie came out to meet him, she was dressed in a light pink beaded dress with long sleeves. Her high-heeled shoes matched the color of the dress. She'd pulled her hair, now in waves, back on both sides. The diamond studs and necklace she'd worn the night before were in her ears and around her neck. Valerie looked lovely.

"Is there any chance we can forget the wedding and stay here. I hate to share you. The bride will be angry when everyone is looking at you."

She laughed. "I had no idea you could be such a flatterer."

"It's no lie. You look amazing."

She smoothed the dress down. "After I've spent this much time getting ready and a fortune on this dress, we're going."

He went to her, slipped his hand around her waist and gave her a soft kiss next to her mouth. "You'll be the most beautiful woman there."

"You know that you don't have to say things like that when no one's around."

"I do if they're true. Everything I say isn't just for show." He didn't like that she had the idea he only said admiring words because of the charade they were playing.

"That's nice to know." She smiled.

"You deserve to be told daily. You should have somebody in your life saying those things all the time."

It wouldn't be him. He wouldn't or couldn't make that commitment. Still, he wished he could.

Owen called for a golf cart. It arrived by the time they made it down the stairs. The drive took them to a chapel built in the woods, not far from the lodge. The building had been constructed completely out of glass, letting the beauty of the outside in. The pews were already filling up, and they were told their seats were at the front on the left-hand side.

Valerie slipped her arm through John's so he could escort her down the aisle. Owen walked behind her proud she was his date. Valerie continued to surprise him. He could hardly

keep his eyes off her. He slid into the pew next
to her along with his extended family. Taking
her hand, he held it during the ceremony. Soon
they were strolling to the reception, which was
being held in a tent on the lawn.

"I love twinkling lights," Valerie murmured. "They're so beautiful."

"Reminds me of Christmas trees," Owen
grumbled beside her.

"There you go being a cynic again." She
gave him a swat on the arm.

"I'm just not that into weddings. I had my
one and never again."

Valerie missed a step and he steadied her.

They looked for their assigned table but
soon learned there was no seating arrangement other than find your own. The wedding
party had place markers, but the rest of the
guests were to mix. They took two empty
seats at a table with a group they didn't know
and soon made new friends. While a small ensemble played in one front corner of the tent
during the dinner, they laughed and enjoyed
themselves.

Owen made a point not to say anything
more about weddings. He'd learned to read
Valerie's body language well enough that
when she tensed, he realized that his comment

about not marrying again had disturbed her, causing her to misstep. Why, he wasn't sure.

After dinner other band members joined the ensemble. People started to move to the dance floor. Owen stood and offered his hand to Valerie. "Would you care to dance?"

A small smile parted her lips as she took his hand. "I don't do much dancing."

"I don't either. We'll do the best we can." He led her to the dance floor.

Owen took her into his arms and whispered against her ear, "I'm really more interested in holding you than I am dancing." They swayed among the other dancers.

"I've told you, you don't have to say things like that when others aren't listening."

"Or maybe I just want you to hear them regardless." He pulled her closer.

Kaitlyn and her husband danced nearby. Owen smiled at her. Kaitlyn's attention stayed more on them than Robert.

At the song change, John cut in and danced Valerie away. She grinned at Owen as she left him on the dance floor alone. Owen couldn't help but feel disappointed not to have Valerie in his arms as he stepped off to the side. He watched as John led her through the dance. The next dance was a faster one. Rich claimed Valerie. Owen heard her laugher as Rich showed off his best moves. She'd won over his sons.

The boys had had their fun. Owen couldn't help but grin. He appreciated that at least the boys liked Valerie and were enjoying their fun at his expense. Just as he moved to reclaim Valerie, Kaitlyn dragged him onto the dance floor. His gaze followed Valerie back to her seat at the table.

Valerie made her way between the tables. She'd enjoyed the look on Owen's face when his boys had whisked her away to dance with them. Earlier her expectations had diminished about her and Owen having anything truly meaningful when he intentionally or unintentionally made it clear theirs wouldn't be a permanent arrangement. She'd begun to hope for more with some of the things he'd said to her, and the way he'd acted. Yet they had only been part of the pretend. She would have to enjoy what she could of Owen this weekend because they would soon be back to the real world.

As she made the last turn to her seat, she noticed a girl of about twelve sitting at a table nearby. Something about her coloring wasn't right. Along with that she was tripoding, sitting with her hands between her legs and leaning forward.

Valerie hurried to her. Pulling a chair close, she sank into it. "Are you okay?"

The girl didn't answer.

The girl's breathing was short and shallow. "Do you have asthma?"

This time the girl looked at Valerie, giving her a slight nod.

"Everything is going to be just fine. I'm a doctor. I'm going to see that you get help. Does your mother have your inhaler?"

The girl looked at her again as she struggled to breath.

"Is she the woman who was sitting beside you?" Valerie had seen the girl earlier with a woman.

"What's going on Val?" Owen's voice came from beside her.

"This child is having an asthma attack."

She looked up. Kaitlyn stood beside him. "Kaitlyn," Valerie said, "I need for you to find this girl's mother. She about five-five, wearing a black dress and has blond hair. Tell her we need her daughter's inhaler right away. We'll be outside the tent."

To Kaitlyn's credit she didn't ask questions but instead turned and headed toward the dancing crowd.

"Owen, we need to get her outside where there is cool damp, air. Bring a couple of chairs." To the girl Valerie said, "Your mother will be here in a minute, but we need to take you outside. It'll help you breathe better. Just walk slowly and take slow, easy breaths. This'll all be over soon." Valerie helped her up and they moved outside the tent.

Owen hurried to set up the chairs. He saw them settled before he announced, "I'm going after my bag. I'll be right back."

Before Valerie could respond, he was gone. Her focus remained on the child. "Just take it easy. Concentrate on slowly breathing in. And slowly breathing out. That's it. Slowly in. Slowly out."

Valerie picked up the girl's hand and looked at her nailbeds. Despite the dim light, she could see that they were getting darker. She glanced inside the tent trying to locate Kaitlyn. *Hurry.*

As if on cue, Kaitlyn came rushing between the tables and then outside with a woman right behind her.

"Oh, God." The woman dropped to her knees in front of the girl, handing her the inhaler.

Valerie placed her hand on the girl's back and slowly rubbed it. "Now take a squirt and breathe deep."

The girl did as instructed. Still, her breathing hadn't improved.

"Once more," Valerie said, encouraging her.

The girl squeezed her inhaler.

Seconds later Owen pulled up next to them in a golf cart. He quickly had his stethoscope in place and listening to the girl's chest. He also checked her pulse and heart rate. He looked at Valerie. "We need to call 911."

"Agreed."

He stood and pulled out his cell phone.

To the hovering mother Valerie said, "We're doctors. I'm Dr. Hughes and this is Dr. Clifton. Your child will be fine, but she still needs to be seen at the hospital."

The child's breathing had improved marginally, but she needed the care only found at a hospital.

The mother said, "Should I take her?"

"No. This is gone on too long. I can't in good conscience let you drive her."

Owen looked at the girl. "We're going to take a little ride to the front of the lodge and meet the ambulance. Dr. Hughes and I will be right beside you. And your mom can go too."

He handed Kaitlyn his phone. "You come along. The hospital is still on the line."

Valerie had to admire her; once again she didn't question. She was her father's child.

They loaded themselves on the golf cart with the girl sitting between her mother and Valerie in the back. Valerie could still hear the child's gasps for air.

At a slow but steady pace, Owen drove them to the lodge.

The mother held the girl while Valerie continued to check her respirations, Owen having handed her his stethoscope when he'd got behind the wheel. They pulled round the corner of the lodge as the ambulance drove up the road using only its running lights.

Quickly they transferred the child to the care of the EMTs. She and Owen gave them a report and the ambulance left.

Valerie heard Kaitlyn say behind her, "Valerie's pretty impressive, isn't she?"

Owen's voice held admiration. "Yes, she is."

CHAPTER SEVEN

OWEN, VALERIE AND KAITLYN rode back to the wedding reception in reflective silence.

At the tent Owen had to explain to the golf cart driver why his cart had been commandeered.

Kaitlyn started toward the tent. "I better let Robert know where I've been. I'm sure he's has been looking for me."

"Kaitlyn, thanks for your help," Valerie called.

"Not a problem. You were both great. I see now why Dad likes you."

Valerie smiled. "I appreciate that."

Kaitlyn waved and hurried off.

Owen leaned into Valerie so he could be heard over the music. "I'm ready to get out of here. How about you?"

"Before the bride and groom leave?"

He winked. "They'll never miss us."

They slid out of the tent without saying any

goodbyes, even to his children. When she asked him about it, he said, "Oh, they'll figure it out. I've got one more night with you, and I'd like some time alone."

"How about taking us the long way around," Owen said to the golf cart driver as he settled in.

The driver nodded and started off.

Owen put his arm around Valerie's shoulders. "You know I was actually envious of my boys tonight."

She gave him a questioning look.

"I was afraid I was going to have to stake claim to my date."

Valerie laid her head on his shoulder. "That's a nice compliment." A few seconds later she said, "I heard what Kaitlyn said to you."

"She's right. You are amazing. In fact, you've been amazing this whole weekend." More than he ever imagined. "You won her over. The boys as well. Me too."

She studied him a moment. "I didn't know I needed to win you over."

"You didn't, but I have to admit I've seen you in a different light." One that he wasn't sure he was completely comfortable with.

"As I have you. We've known each other all these years and how little did we actually know about each other. I think we've grown closer, don't you?"

"I do." He brushed the top of her shoulder with the tip of his fingers. He couldn't stop touching her. Which was an entirely foreign idea for him. Even with his late wife, he had never been overly affectionate in public. Valerie did something to him that he couldn't explain. Yet he found it exciting. He felt more like himself. He was slowly coming back.

Too soon the driver stopped in front of the cabin. Owen cupped her elbow and helped Valerie up the stairs to the porch. "Would you like to sit out here for a while or go inside?"

"I'd like to sit out here, but I'm going to get out of this dress and these heels first."

"I could do without this monkey suit as well. I'll tell you what. I'll fix us a cup of tea while you change."

"You really are a nice man."

He raised his brows. "Was there ever a doubt?"

Owen had just finished brewing the tea when Valerie returned wearing her silk pajamas.

She picked up the mugs. "I'll meet you outside."

He quickly removed and hung up his suit before pulling on a sweater and jeans. Then he went to find Valerie outside with her legs tucked beneath her on the settee. He took the spot next to her. "I'm going to miss this."

"I will too. It's nice and peaceful here."

"Maybe we can come back again sometime." What had him saying things like that? They had made no plans to continue the pretend relationship beyond this weekend.

Valerie placed the mug on the floor beside her. "I'd like that."

Their relationship had moved beyond his control. Oddly, he liked it.

They continued to sit quietly as he finished his tea. Valerie shivered against him. "You're getting cold. Come on, I'm taking you inside and turning on the fire." He picked up both mugs with one hand and with the other helped Valerie to her feet. With a hand at her waist, he nudged her toward the door. She didn't resist. "You go finish getting ready for bed and I'll clean up in the kitchen."

"Are you sure you have those kitchen skills?" she teased.

He quirked a corner of his mouth. "That much I can do." He waited in the living room until she finished in the bathroom. He couldn't help but watch as she dropped her robe and slid under the covers.

What did he do now? He wanted to go to

her. Kiss her. Take her to bed. He was out of practice and couldn't afford to mess this up. He'd always been steady, confident, but this was Valerie.

He would act as normal as possible. As if getting into bed with Valerie happened all the time. Returning from the bath in his boxers, he found the lights had been turned off. The only light came from the glow of the fire in the distance.

Valerie lay on her side facing his side of the bed with her head in her palm. "I was wondering if you were ever going to get out of there."

"Were you timing me?" He climbed under the covers.

"No, but you do have to admit this is unusual for us. The sharing the bed part."

"Which I appreciate you doing. Sharing the bed. Along with other things."

"Not a problem."

He took the same position facing her.

"You know, I've had a crush on you for years." She didn't look at him, her fingers playing with a wrinkle in the sheet.

"I had no idea. I'm flattered." He was. All this time she'd been right there. So near. He couldn't see. He'd been wandering in a fog of half existence until Valerie woke him. Until recently he'd gotten up every day and put one foot in front of the other to make it through the day, with the hope of sleeping a few hours at night. He'd lost his way when Elaine died.

In the last few weeks with Valerie and especially this weekend, he had started to find his way back home. It felt good.

He pushed back a lock of hair that had fallen across Valerie's forehead and cheek. She didn't try to stop him. Instead, she watched him. Her eyelids closed as if she were savoring the movement when his fingers brushed her skin.

"Valerie, I'd like to kiss you. I want to do more but that's not what we agreed on for this weekend. I don't want to mislead you. I like being with you. I want us to enjoy one another, but I can't promise you more. My heart is closed. I just can't care like I once did. I'm not capable of giving you more than the here and now. We're good friends. I believe we would be great as lovers, but I can't offer you beyond that. Will that be enough for you?" He held his breath waiting for her answer.

"You would never mislead me. I trust you. I want this too." Valerie leaned toward him.

Owen didn't pass on the invitation. His mouth found hers. She rewarded him with a sigh. It only encouraged him. He wanted more. All of her. Valerie lay back, sweet and trusting as he rolled to half cover her. Her arms circled his neck and clung to him as their kiss deepened.

She opened her mouth for him. Their tongues did a dance of desire. His need spiraled to a dizzying height. He couldn't be more entangled if she'd cast a net around him. His thoughts, his cravings centered on Valerie.

Owen's hands traveled along her rib cage to her waist. He wanted to touch her everywhere. To experience all of her. To return the pleasure.

He released her lips to have his skim over her cheek to nuzzle at her ear then leave kisses at her temple. "You smell wonderful. Taste even better."

"Mmm, that's always nice to hear." Valerie kissed his shoulder.

His blood ran hot. Had he ever wanted a woman more?

His hand cupped her breast. Valerie pressed into his palm. He fingered a button of her pajama top. "May I?"

"I wish you would."

His fingers worked the button open then moved to the next one. The low firelight flickered off the skin he revealed. As he pushed her top away with the intension of revealing a breast, Valerie's hand stopped him.

"I'm not one of those girls at the hospital who flirt with you. I'm not as young and nimble as I used to be. I don't want you to be disappointed."

"You disappoint me? That never occurred to me. I don't think that's possible. I've only made love to one woman in the last thirty years. I'm the one terrified here."

She cupped his face as she offered him a reassuring smile. "Don't be. I hear it's like riding a bike—it comes back to you."

"I sure hope so because I want you so much I'm willing to make a fool of myself."

Valerie took his hand and placed it over her breast. "Touch me, Owen."

"Your wish is my command." He pushed the slick material back, exposing a luscious globe that made his manhood thicken. He lifted her breast, weighed it before his lips found her nipple.

Valerie's hands went to his hair, her fingers holding him steady as she arched into his mouth. Her moan of pure female passion rippled through him. His length throbbed. He had to have Valerie naked. To see all of her. To have her open to his worship. He released the last of the buttons of her top, pushing it away. He leaned back and admired the feast before him. It had been so long, too long since he'd allowed himself to enjoy a woman's body. His hand trembled as he traced the outline of her nipple. His blood heated at her shiver. Wasting no time, his mouth found her nipple, savoring it, twirling his tongue around the nub until it stood firm.

Valerie moaned low in her throat as she ran her hands across his back and up once more.

He moved from one breast to the other, giving each the same attention. Her breasts were luscious and full. More importantly they were his to explore. He pulled back. "This shirt needs to go."

Valerie lifted off the bed enough for him to remove the concealing clothing. He threw the top to the floor as she pulled him down to her. Her heated flesh meeting his chest had his manhood screaming with need.

As she gave him an open mouth kiss, Valerie's hands ran along his sides and down to his butt. Her fingers slipped under the elastic band of his boxers. They retreated to tease him again as if she couldn't get enough of him. His ego soared. If he doubted his ability to want a woman again, it left with Valerie's gratifying attention.

"These need to go." She pushed at his boxers.

"Say no more."

He climbed out of bed. With a jerk of the covers, he sent them to the end of the bed, leaving Valerie exposed. She pulled a pillow over her.

"Please don't. You are magnificent. All ripe and ready in all the right places. So perfect. Please don't ever hide from me. You're a gift in so many ways."

Valerie's eyes glistened. She removed the pillow. "Now it's your turn."

She didn't have to ask him twice. He shoved his boxers to his ankles and stepped out of them.

Valerie's eyes widened as his manhood came into view. She boldly studied him. He shouldn't have been surprised. With a look of satisfaction, she reached out a hand.

He rejoined her on the bed. His lips found hers again. Could he ever get enough of her nectar? Heavens, he became a sappy romantic poet around Valerie. His hand kneaded a breast as he kissed behind her ear.

Enjoying the silkiness of her skin, his hand brushed over it on the way to the pajama pants waistband. He teased her just as she had done him. Flicking his fingers farther and farther beneath her clothing. She squirmed beneath him.

"Now who has on too many clothes?"

Without a word she lifted her hips off the mattress. Owen tugged until her pants were down. She kicked them away. He sat back taking in the full length of Valerie by firelight. "You are breathtaking."

Valerie watched him with dreamy eyes, but seemed unsure of his estimation.

"I mean it. Scrubs cover up a treasure trove of pleasure."

Her smile turned soft.

He touched her lips with the tip of a finger. Then trailed it along her neck and down her chest to follow the slope of her breast out to the tip. From there he went along her breast to run down her chest. Her muscles rippled as he moved over her stomach. He circled her belly button, causing her to quiver. He kissed her belly button before continuing downward until he reached the nest of curls at the juncture of her legs.

"Owen." His name was little more than a whisper.

His gaze met hers. "May I touch you? I've dreamed of doing so."

She closed her eyes and relaxed her legs.

He lay beside her. His lips found hers as his finger slipped between her folds to find her wet, ready entrance. As his tongue plunged into her mouth, she flexed toward his finger taking all he had to give. She grabbed at his shoulders, her fingers digging into his muscles as she rode his digit. He pulled out and entered again. With a flicker of his fingertip, she tensed. He released her mouth in time to watch her face fill with pleasure. It was the most remarkable moment of his life to have witnessed her come apart in his hands. She finally, eventually lowered to the bed with a long moan that made his heart swell.

He leaned away from her but continued to stroke a finger along the line of her hip.

Her eyes opened. She smiled. "You have talents you've been keeping to yourself, Doc."

Owen chuckled. "Thank you. It's always nice to know when your skills are appreciated."

She propped herself up on her elbow, pushing him down. "And they should be reciprocated. It's my turn to explore."

Her lips found his in a soft kiss that left him wanting more as her mouth moved to his ear. She nipped and tugged at the lobe before kissing his neck. One of her hands bushed his chest hair, moving lower and lower then up again. He needed her to touch his manhood, wanted it.

His breath caught as her hand ran lightly over the length of him.

"You like?"

"Hell, yeah."

He felt her smile against his skin. Taking her hand, he placed it over his manhood. He didn't have to ask for more. Valerie's fingers wrapped him and pumped. Could life get any better than this?

Valerie gave him a deep seductive kiss that had him on the road to losing control. He rolled away and jerked the bedside table drawer open. Pulling out a package, he quickly covered himself. In the next seconds he was above Valerie.

"Are you sure about this?" If she said no, he might die.

She placed her hands on his hips and pulled him to her. "So sure."

Owen plunged into her. Unable to stop himself he plunged and returned. It had been too long and Valerie was too desirable. He couldn't go slow and easy. The need for release was wild and hot. With one more thrust he threw his head back and groaned. He shook, savoring the completion of a powerful moment.

He fell half on Valerie and half on the bed. His face rested in her neck. Her arms came around him. In a soothing motion her fingers moved across his back.

Heaven help him, he'd stepped over into territory he'd never intended to enter. Even now he wanted her again.

Valerie pulled the covers over them. He'd rolled onto his back and now snored, yet his hand still touched her. She'd moved away, but he'd murmured before finding her again. Her heart clung to that, holding tight.

She was in love with Owen. For years she suspected as much, but after this weekend she had no doubt. The bigger question was what could she do about it? Would Owen, or could Owen let himself feel the same?

The ghost of his wife still ran his life. Valerie didn't want him to forget Elaine because their life together had made up so much of who Owen was. But room must be made for him to live again. Here in this bed, they had been living. She wanted that forever.

His fingertips tickled her side. "Hey."

"Hey yourself."

"Sorry I went to sleep on you. Literally and figuratively." His finger traced the line of her jaw.

"Not a problem."

"I'll do better next time." He kissed her shoulder.

"I thought we did pretty good this time."

He chuckled. "For an old man who's out of practice."

"We can work on the practice part. And you aren't old."

"Thanks for the compliment, but I'd like to show you I'm not always so quick on the draw."

She grinned. "Hey, I'm not complaining but you feel free to show off anytime you want."

"Give me a little time to recover and I'll see what I can do."

Valerie kissed his hand when it passed her lips. "Promise?"

"Count it. Come here." He tugged her to him. "I want to hold you. Let's get some sleep."

Valerie tucked into his side in spoon fashion. She wanted this forever. To be wanted. Needed and desired by Owen.

The sun had yet to lighten the sky when Owen woke her. His hand cupped her breast as he nuzzled her ear. "Valerie, I want you."

His need pressed long and hard against her butt. Valerie wiggled against him.

At that invitation, he shifted so she lay beneath him. "This time I promise you'll be treated the way you should be."

She'd had no problem with before, but she would cherish whatever Owen was willing to give for as long as he would. Their time was running short, and she planned to absorb all of him she could.

He kissed her mouth slowly and gently, her toes curling, before his mouth touched her eyes, the tip of her nose. "You're so wonderful. In bed and out. Thank you for sharing yourself with me."

She gripped his biceps as his mouth found her breasts again. He kissed one then the other. "Perfect."

His hand drifted to her stomach. It fluttered in anticipation of his touch.

"Are you ready for me, sweet Valerie?" His finger found her center. He nuzzled her neck. "You are. What a nice reward." He moved away.

"Owen?" She hated sounding so needy. It had been a while for her too. Now that Owen had opened her desire, she was ravenous.

He chuckled. "Just a moment. I'm not leaving you." He opened the drawer again.

"Do you always come prepared?"

"Are you asking if I expected this? No. Rich slipped these in my hand last night." He covered himself.

"I'll have to tell him thank you."

"No, you will not. I'll not have my children involved in my sex life. Now, where were we?" He kissed her. "I believe I found the right place." Sliding over her, Owen said, "Open for me Valerie. I want you sweetheart."

She did as he asked. He slipped inside her as if he belonged. As far as she was concerned, he did. He rose on his hands. Her hips flexed to meet him. His strokes were long and deep. He'd pull away until she feared he was gone before he'd slowly return letting her appreciate every nuance of what he made her feel. He seemed in no hurry.

"Valerie, look at me. I want to see your pleasure." He dipped again.

"Oh."

He did it again. Pressure built in her becoming an untamed, unruly need. She pushed toward him, desire growling at her. Owen kept the steady pace as her hands gripped the sheet. She flexed and begged, head moving back and forth in her demand to have more of him.

His breathing was heavier, but his gaze remained locked with hers. "We're going to do this together."

With quick deep thrusts, he sent her over the edge. She floated into darkness where only Owen's touch existed. Pure bliss like she never experienced before washed through her. He continued moving in her, holding her in paradise. Then slowly she drifted back to the world of Owen howling his own release.

Valerie wrapped her hands around his waist and pulled him to her. She never wanted to let him go.

"Valerie, sweetheart, nothing has ever been as good as you."

CHAPTER EIGHT

VALERIE WOKE TO an empty bed. She ran her hand over where Owen should have been. The sheets were cool. He'd been gone for a while. There was none of the warm cuddling of the morning before. Their heated lovemaking had been even more than that. She pulled the covers up over her naked body.

She looked around the room. The sun shone brightly. It must have been late in the morning. She spied Owen's head on the other side of the sofa in front of a cold fireplace. He must have turned the gas off when he got out of bed. Their lovemaking by firelight had been all she could have dreamed of.

Untangling herself from the covers, she found her PJ jacket, put it on and padded to Owen. She took the seat next to him. He sat with his elbows on his knees and a mug of coffee in his hands that no longer steamed.

Her heart tightened when he continued to

look at the mug, not acknowledging her. This was what she feared the most. She felt her heart cracking. Owen had gone back into his widower shell. She sat there for a moment, fearing what he might say.

Finally, he straightened. He looked at her briefly. "I'm sorry, Valerie."

"What do you have to be sorry for?" If she made light of his attitude, pretend not to know what he meant maybe it would go away. "I had a lovely evening and night."

He shook his head. "I'm sorry, but it can't happen again."

"Why can't it happen again?" Her stomach clenched.

"I just can't." He sounded so miserable. Conflicted.

"Talk to me. Tell me how you're feeling." They had always been able to talk to each other.

He huffed. "All right, if you insist on knowing. I feel like I've been disloyal to Elaine. I never ran around on her. I might've been tempted, but I never crossed that line."

"You're an honorable man. There's nothing wrong with you wanting another woman now that she's gone. We're two consenting adults. We're certainly old enough to know what we're doing. Are you going to live your whole life looking over your shoulder and letting Elaine dictate what you do even though she's nowhere around? I thought the whole point of this weekend was to distract your children. But it turns out it's not them you're really worried about it. It's your dead wife."

Owen's face darkened. He slammed the mug on the table, splashing the liquid over the side. "You don't know what it's like to lose someone."

She'd obviously stepped into an area he wasn't prepared to exam. "No, I've never lost someone to death, but I do know about being left. The hurt, the shame, the humiliation, the disappointment, the loneliness. You aren't the only one who has ever lost someone."

"You think I don't know that? That I don't live with it every day?"

"I know you do. Do you think Elaine would want you to be living alone, feeling guilty every time you enjoyed yourself?"

"Of course not! She'd want me to be happy. But I don't think she would appreciate me going to bed with women."

Valerie liked to think she wasn't just any woman. "You're not going to bed with 'women.' You made love to me. You, we, did nothing wrong." She reached out to touch him.

He flinched and she pulled back. "In fact, we did everything right as far as I'm concerned."

Owen sat straighter. "I didn't mean to imply you did something wrong."

She glared at him. "The part I'm not enjoying is the morning after discussion."

He hung his head. "What I don't enjoy is the guilt I feel."

Her heart softened. Owen looked miserable, but he had to face what he wanted now despite what was in the past. "I know the conflicting feelings you're having must be difficult to deal with. I get that, but you're going to have to figure out what you want. How badly you want it. I'm sorry about Elaine. About your pain. I wish I could make things better for you because your happiness does matter to me. Yet I can't let you hurt me. I promised myself I'd never let that happen again. If you want to feel guilty for something, you should feel guilty about this conversation. I'm going to get dressed. I'll be ready to go in a few minutes."

"I'm sorry, Valerie. Truly I am. I never meant to hurt you. That was never my intent."

"I'm sure it wasn't, but that doesn't mean that it hasn't happened." She moved into the bedroom area.

"I should never have come up with this

crazy scheme of bringing you up here or any-body else for that matter."

"That's true. It's my fault I agreed to go along with you." She was tired of trying to get him to care for her. She had been hurt by her ex, and now Owen had done virtually the same thing for the same reason. His heart belonged to his wife, be she dead or alive. She'd let Owen slip under her defenses.

"What I'm most sorry about is how you feel about the weekend, particularly last night because my memories are wonderful." With that she went into the bathroom and closed the door. She managed to make it that far before tears ran down her cheeks.

Once more she'd had been rejected. She'd let her heart become involved again. Then, bam, it had gotten stomped. She shouldn't have expected any better. That was her destiny being thrown to the side by some man. Why did she think anything would be different with Owen? Love had gotten her nowhere. With her heart crushed and alone once more, was she destined to be the "goodbye girl" forever?

She turned on the shower and stepped under the heated spray.

Owen's loving had been more passionate than she'd ever expected to experience.

What made it so painful was the one man she wanted the most was still hung up on his wife, his dead wife. Nothing Valerie could say or do would ever change that. She refused to live with a ghost. Too many times she'd been pushed away for someone else to take her place. It was time she stood up for herself and demanded she be the center of someone's universe.

Somehow, someway she would try to move their relationship back to the friendship zone. Yet she was confident nothing would be the same. Too much had passed between them in the last few days. There would be no going back. The problem with the rejection this time was it hurt deeper, cut more acutely than it ever had before. Worse than that, she feared it would be a chronic condition for her to always love Owen. He was everything she'd ever wanted in a man: kind, loving to her and his children, funny, charming, considerate, loyal and proud.

Her tears fell with the water. Her hope to find a spot in his life gone like the water down the drain.

Thirty minutes later she stood in the living area with her luggage at her feet. "I'm ready to go when you are."

He'd dressed while she had been in the bathroom. Apparently he was as eager to leave as she, his bags already by the door. She glanced back to bed where she'd spent some amazing hours.

Reaching for her bags, Owen said, "I'll get that for you."

"I can handle it."

He looked like a balloon that had lost its air. "Valerie, it doesn't have to be like this. I'm sorry I hurt you."

She must stand her ground, or she would break down. "I think it does have to be like this. You and I both know from watching surgery, it's better to cut it away with a sharp knife. The dull ones only cause infection and a painful death."

Valerie didn't miss his wince. She'd hit a nerve. She didn't care. Her feelings were hurt as well. Deeply. "Owen, can we go now. I don't want to talk about this any further. We're just going around in circles."

She handed her luggage to the golf cart driver waiting at the bottom of the stairs. The young man placed it on the cart then took Owen's. She sat in the seat closest to the front. Owen moved in beside her but didn't touch her. For that she was thankful. If she could just make it home without falling apart. They came to a halt in front of the lodge. Owen went to see about the car. Now if she could manage not to see his children before they left.

The mother and daughter from the wedding the night before came out of the lodge. Valerie smiled at the young girl. She looked much better than she had at the reception. Valerie took a careful look at her coloring. "How're you feeling this morning?"

"I'm fine." The girl gave her a tentative smile, which was more than she done earlier.

The mother and child walked over to where Valerie stood. "I didn't have time or the mindfulness last night to introduce myself. I am Michelle Warren." She put a hand on the girl's shoulder. "This is my daughter Ashley. I want to thank you for helping her last night. For being so aware of what was going on. You and the other doctor saved her life. We're both very grateful."

Valerie looked at the girl. "You're very welcome. I'm glad I was there when you needed me. Be sure to keep that inhaler with you at all times. It's important."

"I will."

Owen joined them.

"This is Ms. Warren and Ashley from last night."

His demeanor changed slightly to the one she'd seen him use with patients. "Of course!

I'm glad to see you up and about. You certainly look better than you did last night."

The girl smiled, as did her mother. Owen had charmed two more women. "Thank you very much for your help. I don't know what we would've done without it."

Owen looked at her. "I'm glad we were both there." The valet pulled up in Owen's car. "We have to say goodbye now. Take care of yourself."

As the mother and daughter walked away, Owen and the valet loaded the luggage. Valerie opened the front passenger door to climb in.

"Dad. Valerie."

With a sinking heart, Valerie turned to see Kaitlyn hurrying toward them with her arm up. They had almost gotten away.

"I went by your cabin, but you'd already left. I wanted to say goodbye."

Owen joined them beside the car.

Kaitlyn spoke to Valerie. "I just wanted to say thank you for making my dad smile again."

Before Valerie knew what was happening, Kaitlyn had her arms around Valerie pulling her close. Valerie couldn't help but be touched.

Just as quickly Kaitlyn let go then hugged her father. "I'll see you guys back in Atlanta."

Without a word Valerie got in the car. On top of feeling like the dregs in a teacup over the trashed relationship with Owen, now it was made worse by deceiving Kaitlyn and her brothers. This weekend had gone worse than she had anticipated it might.

They had been traveling for an hour when Owen said, "I'd like for us to at least try to be friends."

The pain in his voice pulled at her heart. "I don't know if I can go back."

"Maybe with more time I'll be able to have a real relationship."

She refused to let his sad voice take hold of her good sense. "Owen, I'm in my forties. I'm not waiting on any man anymore. What if you're never ready?" Or she didn't want him anymore when he came around. That wouldn't happen, but she wasn't going to tell him that.

"I just need more time." His tone had turned pleading.

"Take all you want." She laid her head back against the seat. At least if she slept her heart wouldn't hurt.

Owen rubbed his chest. The tightness in it wouldn't ease. He'd figuratively kicked Valerie in the teeth. Now he didn't know what to do about it. He'd been honest with Valerie about how he felt. Even so, she had the right to feel horrible.

He couldn't get away from the memory of their perfect night, of Valerie being warm and snug in his arms. He wanted more of those moments. Thank goodness he hadn't said so out loud. To have led Valerie on more than he already had would be wrong. What had he been doing making love to Valerie when he was still bound to Elaine? All the guilt had washed over him when he woke.

Owen hadn't given up that part of his life completely. He wasn't ready for that. Didn't feel emotionally stable enough yet. Until the last few weeks, his passion had been locked behind a door. Valerie had opened it, releasing a Pandora's box of desires.

He needed to sort through them, but he had to be honest with Valerie as well. She deserved that. Still, that honesty had hurt her. He glanced her. She remained asleep. They had been up most of the night after all. Vivid, sweet moments assaulted him. She looked just as lovely at this moment as when she had dressed for the wedding or when the firelight had reflected off her skin in bed.

Even though he wanted to caress her cheek he wouldn't let himself. She'd shared her pain with him. About how careful she had been with men. Then he'd gone and treated her exactly the same way. She had the right to feel devastated. To have no use for him.

He'd set her at arm's length. No, he'd pushed her across the room, out of the house and down the road. He wouldn't blame her if she never spoke to him again. He'd stepped over the line and lost his friend.

Now his guilt was twofold: Valerie *and* his wife. How could he get past this to regain Valerie's friendship? If he didn't find a way, he'd have lost both of them. The idea of that happening crushed him.

Once they arrived at her condo he offered to carry in her luggage.

"That's not necessary. I've got it." She started up the walk.

"Valerie, is there any way I can make this better?"

She faced him. "Owen, please don't say anything you don't mean. Just leave it alone. We've both said what we feel. We'll adjust and move on."

Feeling gut punched, he said, "If that's the way you want it."

"It is." She started up the walk again then stopped. "Owen."

"Yes?"

"Be kind to yourself." With that she squared

her shoulders and walked to her condo. Without looking back, she closed the door behind her.

Why had that simple action seemed as loud as a ten-foot-thick metal door slamming. Too final. He wanted to run after her, bang on that door and beg her forgiveness. Yet that wouldn't be fair to her.

Valerie had opened up to him. Had shared all of herself and he'd thrown it back at her. It had been a long time since he had been in bed with a woman, but he recognized when someone cared for him. The problem stemmed from the fact that he cared about her as well.

He'd work his way through this. When Elaine had died, he'd had to do the same thing. Stay busy. See the kids more. Visit friends. Play more golf.

Maybe with time, he and Valerie could become friends again. If she agreed. But after the way he treated her this morning he didn't see her ever trusting him again. With the weight of sadness hanging over him, he drove home to his large empty house that offered him no peace.

Valerie breathed deeply before she entered the OR the next day. Monday mornings tended to be overwhelming on the best of days and today it was worse. She would have to face Owen. Even the hours they had been apart hadn't ease her pain. The hardest time had been when she tried to sleep without him. In just a short while her body had begun to crave his warmth.

"Hey, Dr. Hughes," Melissa, the woman behind the department desk said. "How was your weekend?"

Valerie swallowed hard. "It was nice to be off. How was yours?"

The sounds of footsteps drew her attention. She glanced back to see Owen approaching. Had he heard her response? Unable to remember what Melissa said Valerie responded, hoping it was appropriate. She took the OR schedule. "Thanks."

Her hands shook as Owen came to stand beside her. She would get through this. The first time would be the hardest. She didn't meet his eyes. "Good mornin', Owen."

"Mornin', Valerie."

She waved her schedule. "Have a good day." On shaky legs, she somehow managed to walk away without running into anything. Owen's look remained on her as surely as if he'd been touching her on the back.

Inside the scrub room she took a deep breath. Meeting him would get better. Each time easier. It had to. She couldn't live like this until she retired. Should she consider a transfer to an outpatient clinic? But that would be running again. She done that before and didn't want to do it again.

She hated that her life had been turned upside down. It hinged on him, and she didn't like it. She'd known better but let her emotions rule her head. When she had visited his home, she had seen all the signs that he wasn't ready to move on with his life. It wasn't that she didn't know better; she just didn't want to give up his attention. Having it had made her feel whole. She started to believe their story of being involved, had enjoyed it too much. Now she'd let a wonderful night of pretend end her carefully crafted life.

Really, when she thought about it, she should have felt ashamed of how she'd treated him. Maybe she should have been more understanding. He had loved his wife so much he felt disloyal to her. Yet he had treated Valerie with little respect. Still their weekend together had been a nice one up until yesterday morning. More amazing than she ever dreamed possible. That was the problem with dreams. Sometimes they come true then turned into nightmares. She couldn't trust them. Daring to dream was foolish.

* * *

The days dragged. Valerie was grateful for the ones she had off because she didn't have to face Owen. Yet she hated not going in because she didn't get to see him. The pain was double-edged. Her emotions remained in a state of constant flux. Just when she thought she had started to recover, she backslid to where she had started. That happened on the days when she saw Owen the most often.

She had managed to keep him at a distance as much as possible. If he came in the locker room, she left. When he happened to come in the snack room, she made an excuse to leave. The share-a-candy-bar days were over.

Owen gave her as much space as possible as well. He wasn't pursuing her or asking her questions. There hadn't been a call from him. He was respecting her wishes. In an odd way, she wished he wouldn't. She missed him more than she wanted to admit. Her life went along as a long, drawn out, dreary movie in black-and-white. More than once she wondered if Owen was having as difficult a time as she. She liked to think so.

Two weeks passed before they were forced into close proximity. Any anesthesiologist, including fellows, not in the OR were invited, strongly encouraged, to observe a difficult case of a three-year-old who had an extremely larger goiter. These cases made intubation difficult, but this was a very difficult case. Dr. Dale Rhinehart, the head of the department, was the attending on the case. Despite his authority, all were invited to offer suggestions about the procedure. It was a rare case; few of them would see this type of operation but once in their career.

Preparing to do the intubation, Dale offered one of the doctors an opportunity to assist. Valerie smiled to herself when Mark jumped at the chance. She wasn't surprised. The rest of the group gathered in closer. In an effort to make sure she didn't find herself pressed against Owen she moved off to one side. His gaze found hers from where he stood on the other side of the room. Her heart fluttered. She made herself look away. That's when she saw it happen. From her vantage point, she had a clear view of Mark from the side. He palmed a vial of fentanyl and slipped it into his pocket.

Valerie's pulse skittered. Had she seen what she thought she had? In her shock she looked at Owen. Their gazes met and his brows furrowed in question. Her attention returned to Mark.

Surely she had been seeing things. Mark couldn't be the person stealing drugs. He was a good guy, willing to help anytime. He had the makings of a great doctor. Would he do it again? He had to show a count at the end of the surgery. How would he account for the missing drug? Her mind raced with questions.

"Be careful not to obstruct the airway at this point," Dale said.

With everyone except Valerie's attention focused on the deliberate, slow movement of Dale's hands, Mark reached into a different pocket and removed a vial. That was how he was doing it! The count would be good for the number of vials while the amount of anesthetic would only be half.

"Another cc fentanyl."

"Here." Mark removed the clear liquid from the vial with a syringe before inserting it into the port of the IV.

Valerie's teeth clenched. Mark made it look like he had anticipated Dale's need instead of what he was really doing—covering up his theft. Suspicion would fall on the whole team; that wasn't fair. Far worse than that, he might be high while caring for a patient.

Valerie seethed. How dare this upstart of a doctor mislead the entire department into believing he was something he wasn't? The whole situation made her angry. She planned to do something about it. Now.

She hung back, talking about the operation with a few of the other doctors, waiting for the room to clear. She was keeping her eye on Mark, who had volunteered to set the anesthesia area in order. Valerie pretended to look over the supply cabinet.

When only she, Mark and a nurse remained, Valerie said to the nurse, "Sally, would you mind getting a few more intubating kits out of main supply for this room?"

With Sally gone, Valerie stepped over to Mark. "I saw what you did."

"What do you mean?" A flicker of panic filled his eyes before they filled with belligerence.

"I saw you put the vial in your pocket."

"I don't know what you're talking about." He went back to replacing a tubing.

"I believe you do. You have a problem. You need help. I want to help you."

He turned his back to her. "I still have no idea what you're talking about."

She moved up beside Mark, forcing him to look at her. "I think you do. You're too smart. Too good a doctor to waste your life stealing drugs."

"You're wrong." He continued to clear away the equipment.

"I saw you take a full vial and replace it

with a half used one. I know what I saw. I'm going to have to tell Dale. He'll get you help."

Mark leaned toward her. "You're crazy."

"Look, the board is getting ready to start a criminal investigation. When the police get involved, it'll be harder to stay out of big trouble. You need to get ahead of this by turning yourself in."

A snarl curled Mark's lips. All pretense of being innocent washed away. He leaned in closer. "It's your word against mine. All I have to do is put the blame on you. All of the medicine was accounted for."

"Except you put a half-used vial back when you took a full one," she spat. The anger she'd been banking had bubbled up.

"You can tell them that, but I'll say you did it." His voice had taken on a superior note. "It'll be your word against mine."

He was right. She didn't have any way to prove what she saw. Yet she couldn't let it just go by as if she'd seen nothing. That would make her an accomplice. "I'm going to give you a day or two to come clean. Then I'm going to have to say something. I don't want to ruin your career. You can get help for this problem."

Mark's face twisted into a mask of anger, eyes flashing. "You hear me, Dr. Hughes. You say one word about this to anyone, and you'll be sorry. I know people who aren't very nice. If they find out I can't supply them, they will not be happy. You keep your mouth shut. What happens won't make you feel good."

Sally came through the door. She and Mark quickly separated.

Valerie's entire body shook as anger ran hot through her. She helped Sally put away the supplies then left. She never would've dreamed she'd be involved in this type of situation. To be threatened made it terrifying.

She stalked down the hall. It wasn't until Owen spoke that she noticed him. He took her arm, stopping her. A shot of electric awareness rippled through her.

"Hey, are you okay? Did something happen in the OR? I saw the look in your eyes."

"I can't talk about it here."

She and Owen may be having their own problems, but she needed someone she could trust. Owen. She knew it as surely as she knew her name. He cared about his patients, this hospital, his family and her. Right now, she needed him.

"Come in here." He pulled her into an empty OR that hadn't been sterilized for the next operation. "What's going on? You look like you're scared to death."

"I can't believe it. Mark is the person who's been stealing the drugs. He says he's selling them to someone, but I suspect that he's an addict." She wrung her hands as she told Owen the entire story of what happened in the OR. "To top it off he threatened me!" She paced the room and back again.

Owen's face had darkened. "He did what? I'm going to find him right now. I'll see him arrested."

Valerie appreciated his solidarity.

He started for the door but she caught his hand. "Wait. You can't do that. We have to catch him in the act. He's right, it's his word against mine."

"They say it tends to be the person who is extra helpful and eager who is able to steal because those are their opportunities to do so." Owen's jaw muscle jumped.

"Yeah, but I would never have thought Mark could be that person. He would be the last person I would've imagined. Sometimes I'm not as good a judge of character as I would like to be."

Owen wasn't sure if that remark had been meant for him, but he felt the punch just the same. "We need to formulate a plan. If it's going to come down to his word against yours, then we'll need to do something to catch him in the act."

Valerie shook her head. "This isn't your problem. I saw him. I confronted him. I'll see about it. You shouldn't get involved."

"If you're involved then I am too."

"Why should you be?"

"Because you're my friend. You need help." He wanted to say more, but he wasn't sure what he should say. "I'm going to talk to Dale. Let him know we need to meet him off-campus to talk about this. I don't want Mark to get the idea you told anybody."

"I don't need your help. I can talk to Dale. I can take care of myself."

Owen's pressed his lips together as he looked at her. "That may be so, but in this case I think you can use all the help you can get. I'm not going to let anything happen to you."

"I still don't understand why."

She just didn't get it. He cared but he couldn't say that. "Let's just say that I don't like to know that my friends are being threatened."

She threw up her hands. "All right."

"Now that's settled, I want you to go to the locker room and get your purse. Don't bother to change clothes. Head straight home. I'll speak to Dale. You don't want Mark to even have a hint that you might tell anyone."

"Don't you think you're overreacting a bit?"

He gave her a stern look. "No. Drug addicts can get desperate. Unpredictable. At home keep your doors locked, pull all the curtains closed and don't open the door to anyone."

A stricken look covered her face. "Okay."

He studied her a moment in disbelief. "You're going to do what I asked without an argument?"

"Yes. You think I should be cautious so I will be."

The relief that went through him wasn't measurable it was so great. "Thanks, Valerie. I'm glad you're taking this seriously."

"I have to admit he scared me."

Owen didn't like the sound of the quaver in Valerie's voice. He fisted his hands so tight his knuckles turned white. The idea of Valerie being threatened by anybody, but in particular Mark, who they both had admired and trusted, made him livid. He had a hard time believing it, but he couldn't ignore what Valerie said she saw. It wasn't something she would lie about.

Regardless of the gulf between them for the last two weeks, he couldn't ignore his need to protect her. If he could, he'd put a indestructible bubble around her. Whether she liked it or not. Something in him he'd never experienced before came to the surface when she'd been telling him about being threatened. He'd always been a peaceable man, but right now he'd like to beat Mark to the floor.

Two hours later, Owen opened the restaurant door, allowing Valerie to enter ahead of him. Dale was meeting them there. He'd been curious about the request, but Owen had said he would explain over dinner. His boss had no idea that Valerie would attend as well. Owen didn't want Dale to accidently say something that he shouldn't.

Owen's idea had been for it to look as if their group had gotten together for an impromptu meal between longtime coworkers in case anyone saw them together. He wouldn't be surprised if Mark was watching Valerie. At this point he wouldn't put anything passed him. Owen feared that she had said enough that Mark might be provoked into doing something horrible.

Owen found Dale sitting at a table in the back corner and led Valerie there. They took their seats and placed orders. Dale then looked between them before he said, "Exactly what's this about? Are you going to tell me you're dating?"

"No!" Owen and Valerie said at the same time.

Dale sat back. "Apologies. I must have misread that. That's what I get for listening to department gossip."

Owen was surprised that he didn't actually mind the idea of being the object of department gossip. In an odd way, he wished he and Valerie were. At least they would be friends again. He glanced at Valerie who fiddled with her napkin. He cleared his throat. "Valerie needs to tell you what she saw today. Then you'll understand."

She wasted no time in sharing in detail what had occurred between her and Mark.

Dale shook his head when she finished. "He's right. It's his word against yours. He could just as easily accuse you. Confronting him isn't the answer. We have to outsmart him."

"I've given that some thought. I wondered what you think about this." Owen looked at Dale as he laid out his plan. "What if we changed the label on a paralyzing drug. While Mark is preparing for a patient, he's left alone. That would be his opportunity to grab the drug. Instead of him shooting up with fentanyl, he paralyzes himself. He wouldn't get hurt, but we could catch him red-handed when he couldn't move. He couldn't deny what he'd done. Plus we'll take pictures and document what we did."

Valerie smiled. The first Owen had received in a long time. "That's quite ingenious. You have a sinister mind."

"Thank you. I'm glad I could impress." And he was. It had been too long since he received a compliment from her, or her even act as if he was worthy of praise.

Dale leaned back in his chair. "That just might work. The question is how do we know when to set him up?"

Owen grinned. "You make the assignments. In a couple of days assign him to me. I'll make sure he goes after the vials."

"Hey, you can't leave me out or he'll know I've said something. It has to happen naturally."

Owen touched her arm. "I don't want to take any chance of you getting hurt."

"I'm not going to get hurt. Mark is more likely to do it in my OR because he knows he has the upper hand around me."

Owen's jaw tightened. "You can't take that chance."

"If you can I can."

"Uh, hum." Dale brought their attention back to him. "Let me handle the placement of Mark. You two just be prepared for him when the time comes. Keep a low profile for the next few days. Be as normal as possible. Valerie, let him believe he has you under control. If we rush this, we might lose our only opportunity."

"That's a good idea," Owen said.

Valerie nodded.

Dale continued, "I'm going to notify the board about what's going on. I don't want anything negative coming back on the department." He gave them a pointed look. "There can be no heroics. I don't want anybody getting hurt. Neither of you and certainly not the patients."

"Agreed." Owen looked at Valerie, who nodded. She was being too quiet. She was either scared or planning something of her own. Which she better not be.

"There's one more thing." Dale looked directly at Valerie. "I'm concerned about his threats. I don't think you should be alone any more than necessary. I'm going to see about one of the security guys staying with you at night."

Valerie jerked forward. "I don't need—"

Owen stopped himself short of taking her hand and holding it. "I've got that covered."

Valerie's mouth opened and closed like a fish.

"I'll be staying with her."

CHAPTER NINE

VALERIE AND OWEN said their goodbyes to Dale before she turned on Owen outside the restaurant. "What made you say that in front of Dale? You're not going to stay with me."

"Then you can stay with me," Owen shot back. "Either way I'm not leaving you alone until this is over. Mark threatened you. That's enough for me."

She didn't want to admit to herself or him that she would feel safer if somebody was with her. Looking over her shoulder all the time wasn't fun. She huffed. "All right, you can come to my place."

In his car a few minutes later Valerie said, "Now that I think about this more it's ridiculous. Mark is not going to come after me. Not in that kind of way. I don't need a babysitter."

"Too late. You've already issued the invitation. You can't take it back."

She couldn't help but smile. Something that

had been difficult to do in the last few weeks, and with this situation with Mark it didn't look like life would get better.

"Like I've said, you never know what he might do. Until Mark is caught, then you're with me or you're at work. I went by my house before I picked you up to get some clothes and toiletries."

She groaned but didn't bother to complain further. Everything about Owen's demeanor and tone said he would have his way.

At her condo she flipped on the lights and dropped her purse in the chair. "You know where the bath is. The extra bedroom is across the hall from it."

"I promise to be a good houseguest." He hoped to cajole her into accepting his presence.

"I wish you weren't here."

Owen placed his hand over his heart. "How inhospitable of you."

"I'm sorry. That did sound awful, and very ungrateful. I'm glad to have someone here with me."

"Just not me."

She studied him a second before she turned to leave the room. He was right and she hated to admit it.

A few minutes later she walked into the living room headed for the kitchen to find Owen wandering around looking at her pictures and examining a wooden box that had been her father's. Having him touch her things seemed so personal, as if he had done the same to her. "I'm going to have a cup of tea. Do you want one?"

He said without turning around, "That'd be nice. You have a great music collection. Do you mind if I put something on."

"I guess not."

His face tightened and brows narrowed. "I'm not here to make you miserable. If you don't want me to play music, just say so. If it would make you more comfortable, I'll go to my room."

"You're right. I'm sorry. No, don't go to your room."

Owen picked out a jazz record and put it on. He sat on the couch. How fast life changed. Valerie could barely tolerate having him around, and it hurt deeply.

A few minutes later she sank into a chair near him. "I still can't believe this. How wrong I was about Mark."

"I like to think I'm a fair judge of character."

She looked into her teacup. "Do we ever really know others? Isn't that why we get hurt?"

Owen shifted his feet. "Are we talking about Mark now?"

Her gaze met his. "Maybe not."

"I know I hurt you. I hate that I have to be here making you uncomfortable. I wouldn't be if it wasn't necessary." His eyes were sympathetic.

Her lips thinned into a line.

Owen went over to sat in the chair next to hers. He leaned forward, giving her a pleading look. "Hey, I didn't mean that like it sounded. In fact, I've missed you."

"Owen—"

"The fact is if Mark is capable of stealing drugs, then he's capable of doing other things to protect himself."

"You can't stay forever." He'd disrupted her life far too much already.

"I don't know that forever will be necessary. What I do know is I'll be here until Mark is caught. I realize there are problems between us, but let's put those aside until we handle this one. Regardless of what has happened or hasn't happened between us, I still care about your welfare."

He just didn't want her heart.

Owen looked down to the end of the hall at the bedroom door firmly shut against him. It was closed as resolutely against him as her attitude had been for the last few weeks. He couldn't blame Valerie. Yet he hated himself for the way their relationship had deteriorated.

That was fine. He was here for a colleague who needed help. He would do what he was doing for anyone. Hell. Now he had started fooling himself. He was here because of Valerie being in danger. She wasn't just any colleague. Valerie meant more to him than that.

He didn't care to examine how much more important. If something happened to her, he would be devastated.

Owen hadn't hesitated to insert himself into Valerie's life, and condo. He had a mission. No one would hurt her if he could prevent it. He didn't think being a man on a white charger was part of his personality, but apparently it was.

When he'd entered her home, he'd dropped his bag and wondered around looking at her belongings. Everything was neat and tidy. The kitchen had a long counter, which included barstools. The space looked adequate but was nothing in size compared to his kitchen. Valerie deserved more than what she allowed herself. She had a wonderful stereo system and great taste in music.

Now he had to try to sleep with her just

steps down the hall when all he wanted was to knock on the door and ask if she would like to dance. He lay down with his hand behind his head, listening to the sounds of Valerie moving around in her room.

What would it be like to experience this each night? One of the aspects he liked about being married was having another person around him, being a part of someone else's life. He had been lonely for so long. Maybe that's why he had latched on to Valerie so easily.

He hadn't found real sleep since the night he and Valerie had made love. His arms craved her now. How many times had he relived those moments? Wished he had them back. Still his guilt held him prisoner.

A noise at his door made him look up. Valerie headed toward the living room.

She jumped when he came up behind her. "It's just me."

"I guess I'm more spooked than I thought. I can't seem to go to sleep." She turned on a lamp beside the sofa. "I didn't mean to wake you up. I was going to get something to drink."

"I wasn't asleep so you're not bothering me. How about watching some TV until we get sleepy? Work a puzzle? Play a game of cards?" Anything to spend time with her.

"An old movie might do it." She turned on the TV and flipped the channels, finding a black-and-white movie. "Do you want popcorn and something to drink?"

"Sure."

She soon had a bowl filled to the top with popcorn, and brought Owen a cold drink. When she started to sit in a chair, he said, "I can't reach the popcorn from over here."

Instead, she headed to one end of the couch and set the bowl between them.

Valerie made sure the boundaries remained defined. Wasn't he the one to blame? He shouldn't complain. It wasn't fair to give her mixed signals, pushing then pulling her back again. Yet he couldn't stay away from her.

He tried to focus on the movie as much as possible. Once he reached for popcorn at the same time as she did. The hot sizzle of awareness rippled through him at their touch, leaving him with a desire he couldn't act on. How little it took to make him want her.

She jerked her hand away.

He made himself focus on the movie. Glancing at Valerie, he found her head lolling to the side. She'd fallen asleep. He placed one of the decorative pillows from the sofa on his thigh then gently guided her head to rest on it. She pulled herself into the fetal position with a sigh. Tugging the throw off the back of the sofa, he spread it over her.

Owen continued to watch the movie, much happier than he had been when she wasn't within touching distance. He let the TV roll into another movie but turned the volume down. Soon he drifted off to sleep.

Too many nights he hadn't slept. Tonight, he would. Because Valerie lay next to him.

Valerie woke unsure where she was. Something heavy lay across her shoulders. She recognized that noise. It was Owen snoring. How had her head ended up on a pillow?

She and Owen had slept on the sofa. Where was her pride? First chance she got she snuggled up to him. As if they couldn't be separated. She looked up to find Owen with his head back on the sofa and his eyes closed. He'd have a crick in his neck when he woke.

She didn't need to add more to her agenda where Owen was concerned. When this business with Mark was over, they would go back to the way things were. Polite, but distance friends. Not that she was excited about that. She'd been more miserable then than when they weren't talking to each other.

He needed to understand she wouldn't be falling into bed with him just because of his proximity. Not that he had asked her to. He had abided by her wishes and kept his distance, been a gentleman. She'd like to think he had been as unhappy as she, but she couldn't tell that by his actions.

Slowly easing out from under his arm, she sat up, stiffly.

"Hey," a rough-edged voice said.

She hadn't been stealthy enough not to wake him. "You should've woken me and told me to go to bed."

"I was just glad you were sleeping."

"You'll certainly need to get some good rest tonight after sleeping on this sofa."

There was still some time before they should be at the hospital. She went to the kitchen, started the coffee maker then pulled out flour and eggs and milk. Her way of dealing with anxiety was to bake. Owen was the definition of anxiety for her.

Fresh bread was in order. There was something about kneading dough that soothed her nerves. She had made a lot of it in the last two weeks. To the point she had a freezer full, and the neighbors had begged her to stop bringing them any because they were getting fat. She hadn't taken all of it to the hospital because she didn't want it to get around how much bread she was actually making. People would wonder why.

Now her frustration lay on her couch. Yep, she needed to make some bread.

She filled a bowl with ingredients. It felt good to have her hands active when she wanted to put them all over Owen. Just more thoughts she shouldn't be having.

In a few hours she would have Mark to deal with. She might believe Owen was overreacting by staying with her, but it did make her feel securer knowing he was there. Dealing with Mark or that type of crime wasn't something she was familiar with.

Her back remained to the living room as she punched a roll of dough down before putting it into a greased bowl. Strong arms circled her waist bringing a yelp from her. Warm lips touched the skin behind her ear. That was her soft underbelly. The spot that made her melt every time.

Her eyes drifted closed as she leaned back against the hard wall of Owen's chest. After a moment she gathered her wits and pulled away. "Please don't do that."

His arms dropped away. "I'd like to say I'm sorry, but I couldn't resist. You look so adorable standing in a cloud of flour."

She settled her voice, finding a nicer tone. "Just don't do it again."

"I can't promise that either." As if he hadn't heard what she said he looked around her. "What're you doing?"

"I'm making bread."

"At this hour?" He looked toward the window. "It's not even daylight."

"It's my stress reliever."

"Hang in there, it's all going to be okay in a few days, I think."

Yeah, but not where he was concerned. After this stay it might even be worse.

"Well, at least it's useful. Unlike other things you could do. Do I get any?" He looked hopeful.

"Maybe if you behave. Now move out of the way so I can get cleaned up. Coffee is ready."

He gave the bowl a hopeful glance. "Aren't you going to bake it?"

"It has to rise. I'll get ready for work and put it in the machine. It'll be ready when I get home this evening." She gave the dough an overly zealous punch.

"Don't you mean when we get home?"

"Yeah, you too." The idea made her nervous.

He took her hand. "Can't we be friends again?"

She studied him a moment. "Nothing has really changed, has it?"

Owen took a moment before he said, "I guess not."

Valerie shook her head sadly. "There's coffee. Have all you want. Make yourself at home."

Thirty minutes later, Valerie joined Owen in the living room.

He said, "I'll drive this morning."

"No, I'll drive. We'll tell anyone who asked that you had car trouble and I picked you up." She needed some control over her life.

"Okay. If that's the way you want it."

As they entered the hospital he whispered, "Remember, don't antagonize or let yourself be by alone with Mark. Take no chances."

She nodded.

His fingers tangled with hers. "I know you don't believe this, but I do care about you. I don't want to see you hurt for anything in the world."

Valerie's heart swelled as ripples of warmth flood her. "I appreciate that."

To her surprise, the day went smoothly.

Mark acted as if nothing had happened between them. His smile was as bold and bright as ever. He asked to help, but she never saw a false move out of him. Maybe their talk had made some headway. That was until she passed him in the hall when no one else was around. His eyes narrowed in a glare, making it clear he remembered their conversation.

Valerie shuddered and continued walking.

On the way home she told Owen about what happened.

"At this point I'm not surprised by anything."

"I'm fine."

"I know you are. I just wish it was me instead of you. I hate for you to be his focus. Still, let's try not to think about him tonight. How about dinner and a movie?"

"It's been a long day. I'd prefer to cook. Takes my mind off of having all this nervous energy."

"A home-cooked meal would be a real treat for me."

A couple of hours later they sat at the counter finishing their meal. Owen had never felt more at peace. There was something right about having a good meal, with a woman he liked in a cozy home. He missed the intimacy.

"This bread is truly amazing." He held up the last of his third slice. "Why haven't I had more of it? I guess the rest of the staff gets to it before me."

"Maybe you're just not paying attention."

"Do I miss so much around me or just things about you? I'm sorry. I should have been a better friend."

She touched his arm briefly. "Don't worry about it. You've been in a bad place for a long time. You're being a great friend now."

The next evening, Owen sat in his car waiting on Valerie to exit the restaurant. He had begged her to make an excuse not to attend the baby shower, but she insisted on going. The nurse who was expecting was one of her favorites. Valerie assured him she would stay with the crowd and not leave until he had texted her he was outside so he could follow her home.

He would have driven her to the event, but she didn't want anybody asking questions about them. This time he was the one bothered by her trying to hide him. He didn't have to imagine how she must've felt when he'd treated her that way. He didn't appreciate it a bit. Truly resented it.

She'd left him standing in the kitchen the night before, sure the last few minutes had been another crossroads in his life, and he'd chosen the wrong road. Again. He wasn't sure he liked that Owen.

She then said goodnight without inviting him to her bedroom. It saddened him that she was seeing to it they remained distant. He had hoped they'd made some progress back to their friendship. She had made it clear she wouldn't be having any more physical contact than necessary. He'd crushed her heart and was paying for it.

While Valerie remained safely inside the restaurant, he'd driven to his house to pick up more clothes and to check on things. His footsteps echoed inside the house. He'd never noticed that before. The warm comforting place it had once been had turned cold. The smell of cooking, the hum of life, or soft music playing weren't there. They were at Valerie's. Here it was nothing but a huge empty house. It wasn't a haven of peace anymore.

Since Elaine died, he'd let the house remain as a monument to her. He hadn't moved a picture or a trinket in five years. If someone moved something, he moved it back to where she'd left it.

He walked into his den. The area that had always been his. It, like the rest of the house, hadn't changed since Elaine had died. Owen shook his head. She owned the room more than he did. All this time he'd been fooling himself.

It was as if his world had stopped. Then he asked Valerie to be his pretend girlfriend, and the world started to spin once more. He'd started to breathe again. His heart started to beat. He'd started to dream, hope, and wish for more than work and to exist. He had an interest in his life. All of that because of Valerie.

He trudged upstairs to his room, his and Elaine's room. He stopped in the middle and turned around. He looked at her portrait. "Elaine, it's time I moved on. I'll always have the memories of our years together. Our children are a precious gift you have given me. I know you would want me to be happy. Please wish me the best."

Owen gathered the clothing he needed. With lighter steps than he'd had in years, he headed down the stairs and out the door. It felt odd but wonderful to look forward to life. For too long he had been going through the motions. His insides rippled with nervous excitement.

Leaving through the kitchen with a new attitude, he stopped to looked around. Valerie needed something like this instead of the small kitchen in her condo. She would bring it to life.

Before he climbed into his car, he looked at the house that was no longer his home. He didn't need its support anymore. His children came but never stayed a long time. They had moved on with their lives. It was time he did the same. This weekend he would call a Realtor and see about putting the house up for sale.

Arriving back at the restaurant, he'd parked where he could see the door and the parking lot. Texting Valerie, he let her know he was outside.

She returned:

I'll be out in a few minutes.

As good as her word, she exited the restaurant along with a couple of other ladies, chatting as they walked over to their cars. Once Valerie pulled away, he drove up behind her and followed her home. As they entered the condo, he said, "I've decided to sell my house."

She turned. Surprise ringing clear in her voice. "Why?"

"I don't need it anymore. It's too big. Lonely."

"Why now?"

He shrugged. "It just seemed like too much when I went home. Like it was time to make a change."

Valerie pursed her lips and nodded. "I'm glad for you, Owen." She continued down the hall to her bedroom and closed the door.

He stared at her door. That wasn't the reaction he'd expected. Why had he thought she would care either way? Why did it matter?

CHAPTER TEN

BETWEEN OWEN LIVING with her and waiting on Mark to make a move, Valerie's nerves grew taut with apprehension. She'd spent the last two nights hanging out in her room so she wouldn't get used to Owen being so close. Keeping him at a distance was the only way to protect her heart from further hurt.

When he'd announced he planned to sell his house, she'd been shocked. Should she read something more into it? What had him making such a huge change? Had he started to see that he'd been existing instead of living? Or had something else brought it on? Whatever it was, selling the house would be a big step for him. She wished him the best, but to keep her sanity she couldn't be more involved than that. Even if she wished she could.

After all, that really wasn't her business, but somehow, he made her feel that his decision might've been related to her. Yet when she'd given him the opportunity to say something he hadn't. She intended to stand up for herself and what she wanted. Never again would she give without getting. Too often she'd been let down.

She didn't want to think of Owen as one of those people, but he'd already done it once. What made her think he wouldn't do it again? Yet he had shown such concern for her. Enough he had interrupted his life to stay with her. She didn't trust her judgment enough to know his true motives. After all, she believed Mark was a good person. She certainly had been misled by her ex, and just a few weeks ago Owen had disappointed her. What she needed from Owen was a grand gesture. Proof that she mattered.

The problem remained that her heart was involved. Owen carried it around with him. He just didn't know it. Or maybe he did, and he didn't care.

She entered her kitchen to see Owen with his butt against the counter, ankles crossed and coffee cup in hand. He looked at home in her small condo. Too much so for her comfort.

"Mornin'…" The soft rumble of his voice made her tingle. Moments like this were what she dreamed of the most. Had wanted all her life. The feeling of belonging and being wanted. She couldn't help but wish for this every day.

"Good morning." She gave him a bright smile. It was nice to get up with another person. Especially Owen. She'd known the first time she'd snuggled against his warm body her life would never be the same. But she couldn't trust this feeling. He would be gone when Mark was caught.

"You know I've had about enough of this."

Owen's eyes lost their glimmer and narrowed. "Are you referring to me or what's going on at the hospital?"

"At the hospital." She wasn't rude enough to say it included him.

His body relaxed and his eyes brightened. "Hey, it'll be over soon. Mark won't last long before he'll need to get a fix. Just hang in there."

"I hope so. If that doesn't happen soon, I'm going to need to be on anxiety meds."

Owen placed a reassuring hand on her shoulder, giving it a gentle rub. "You've got this."

It was a nice reminder he was in her corner regardless of her efforts to shut him out. With the exception of her family, she'd never experienced that before. For Owen's support she would always be grateful.

Before they entered the hospital, he once again reminded her of the need to remain calm and to take no chances. "I've got your back."

She pulled the door open. "Who's got your back?"

"He might take it if he's in my OR, but I doubt it. Unfortunately, I expect he's going to do so in yours. Especially because he thinks he can control you since no one else has questioned him. As grueling as the last few days have been, we've given him a false sense of security. He believes his intimidation worked. He's feeling safe."

She hadn't thought of it that way. With that security he'd be more likely to act.

"Go have a good day."

"After that little speech, how's that supposed to happen?" She started down the hall toward the surgery department. Owen followed.

With a wry smile, he said, "Okay, the best day you can."

"I'm already looking forward to tomorrow. I need the day off." She could use a day away from the hospital.

"I'm off too. Do you want to do something together? Maybe a round of golf?"

"Owen, I don't think that's a good idea.

Nothing has really changed between us." She couldn't keep acting like he wasn't hurting her with their togetherness.

"I'm sorry. You're right. It won't happen again." He didn't look happy with the decision.

It was midafternoon, and Valerie's last case when Mark entered the OR. Even with a mask on she could tell he had a smile on his face. The humor in his eyes changed when he met her look. They became serious with an edge of desperation. This was it. Today he would be stealing again. She would bet money on it. The medicine sat on the table beside her, waiting for him. She just had to keep her cool and not give anything away.

He spoke to those in the OR then came up beside her. "I've been assigned to this case with you."

Valerie swallowed. She stilled her shaking hands. This would be his opportunity, and she would give it to him. Lifting the IV line, she checked it. "I'll do the injection if you want to handle monitoring the gas."

He lowered his head, giving her a direct look. In a low voice he said, "I'd rather do the injections."

She received the message loud and clear. He wanted his drugs. She nodded.

"I like working with you." He made sure to say it loud enough that the others heard it.

Valerie wished she could say the same. Now it was her job to see that her patient came to no harm while trying to catch Mark. She watched him closely but never saw a wrong move. Occasionally they made eye contact. Each of them performed the duties necessary to keep the patient asleep and pain free.

The surgeon had almost completed his job when Mark said, "I need more fentanyl."

This was her chance. Valerie's heart rate picked as she handed the bottle she'd prepared for this moment to Mark. She had watched close enough to know the patient had plenty of pain medicine in his system.

Not actually seeing Mark put the vial in his pocket, she had no doubt he had done so. He filled a needle from a vial that was half-full. She had handed him one that was full. He filled a cc of the liquid and put it into the IV line. The extra cc wouldn't hurt the patient or Valerie would have stopped him.

With a satisfied look in his eyes, he placed the vial on the table beside her. He had gotten what he wanted. Valerie all but held her breath until the procedure was complete, fearing something would go wrong. She'd tried her best not to watch Mark too closely.

With the surgeon finished, Mark volunteered to see the patient to recovery. Valerie was good with that. With her blood racing, she searched for Owen and Dale.

Dale wasn't in his office. Panic welled. She had to find help. On her way to the department desk, she saw Owen approaching. She nodded, her look not leaving his.

When he reached her, she grabbed his arm. "He took the bait."

"He did! Let's just hope he uses it here." Excitement flashed in Owen's eyes.

She looked down the hall. "We have to find him. He'll disappear to shoot up. Where's Dale? We'll need security."

They walked to the department desk. "Have you seen Dale?"

"I think he's finishing up a case in OR three."

They started that way when Dale exited the room. The look on their faces must have given them away.

"Where is he? I'll get security." Dale took long strides toward his office.

She and Owen quickly followed him. "We don't know. He went to recovery and hasn't returned."

"Then we need to find him. I wondered how much longer it would be before he went after it again. I'll call security. You two stay out of this." Dale continued down the hall.

"Come on, Valerie." Owen took her arm. "We'll wait at the department desk. I don't want you to be by yourself if Mark happens to realize you gave him the wrong drug and comes looking for you. If only half our plan works, he could still be dangerous."

"Shouldn't we look too?" She started down the hall away from the department desk.

Owen's grip tightened. "No." His word stopped her. "We're going to do what Dale said. Security will handle it from here."

"Okay. But I'm not hiding." She lifted her head before turning toward the other end of the hall. Valerie had never had somebody protect her as vigorously as Owen. She liked the feeling of being a priority to him. Something she'd never been to any man in her life.

Minutes later she watched from the desk as Dale met two large security guards when they entered the department. If they were going to catch Mark, they had to find him soon. The medicine would be starting to take effect by now. They didn't dare have him recover before he was located. She needed peace of mind. Today this had to end.

The guards methodically went from room to room. Soon they entered the break room.

She could only wait for their return. Owen moved closer. She appreciated the reassurance. They waited. Waited.

"Shouldn't we go see what is happening?" She took a step forward.

Owen took her elbow. "Let them do their job. You've more than done yours."

"He's right." Dale continued to watch the door through which the security guards had disappeared. The time clicked by on the large industrial clock on the wall above the desk. A crowd of curious staff gathered around them. The guards usually steered clear of surgery.

"What's going on?" people asked from behind them.

Valerie held her breath. The guards were taking a long time. They must have found him. She clutched her hands in front of her. Soon this would be over. Then her life would return to what it was. No Owen there every day. Sadly.

One of the security guards stuck his head out of the break room door. "We found him slumped over on the floor by the bathroom."

The group started toward the break room. Valerie's heart jumped. She raised her chin. "I'm not missing a minute of this. I've earned it."

They entered the break room to find Mark

lying on the floor. His eyes were open, and he could hear everything happening but couldn't move. One of the guards came out of the restroom with a plastic bag in hand. Inside was the vial Mark had taken from her in the OR along with a syringe.

The air whooshed out of her and strong arms wrapped around her waist. Owen lifted her into the air.

Without a thought Owen grabbed Valerie and pulled her to him. His mouth found hers. "We did it."

At her startled look, he glanced behind them to see the staff watching them with a mixture of surprise and smiles.

Valerie gave him a gentle push. "Everyone is watching."

"I don't care." His lips found hers again for a quick kiss.

This time the staff clapped. There were even a few hoots.

He'd been more worried about Valerie than he realized. It wasn't until Mark had been caught that he recognized how much. Now he didn't care who knew it anymore. If Mark had harmed her, he didn't know what he would have done.

He looked at Valerie. Her eyes were wide,

her cheeks flushed. She never looked more beautiful. He was in love with her. The realization should have scared him to death, but instead he felt alive again.

Dale cleared his throat. "The police are going to need statements from you two." He directed his attention to the crowd. "Everyone else please get back to work."

The staff members slowly exited the room.

Owen nudged Valerie out of the way as the guards lifted Mark into a chair.

"He'll be all right in a few minutes," Dale assured the guards. "Have the police come back here to get him." He turned to Owen and Valerie then smiled. "You two make a good team. Nice work. As soon as the police have finished with you, take off. I can handle anything else." He gave them each a knowing look. "Enjoy your evening."

Valerie's face pinkened again.

Owen stayed close to Valerie as she told the police what happened, then he had his turn. Dale assigned a nurse to sit with Mark as he came out of the drug.

"You ready to go?" Owen asked Valerie.

"Past. I'll get my purse."

On the drive home they said little. After his acceptance of his feelings for Valerie, he needed to take a moment to think about them. He wouldn't be surprised if Valerie sent him home. He had no doubt she would chastise him for kissing her. She'd been diligent about keep her distance. Would she listen or believe him when he told her how he felt?

He'd hurt her deeply with his rejection. How could he make that up to her? He had to find the right time to discuss it with her. Now wasn't it. They were emotionally drained. There would be a better opportunity.

A few minutes later he followed her into the condo.

Valerie dropped into a chair, leaned her head back and closed her eyes. "What a day."

"I couldn't agree more." Owen followed her example and flopped on the couch.

Neither of them talked for a few minutes then Valerie said, "You kissed me in front of everyone."

His chest tightened. Opening his eyes, he looked at Valerie. Hers remained closed. There was a tenseness to her despite her relaxed posture. "I did."

"Why?" She still didn't look at him. "I thought you didn't want anyone talking about you, us." She shrugged. "Then again there is no us."

"I want there to be an us," he said softly.

Valerie's eyes opened. "You do?"

"I do. I kissed you because I was relieved you were out of danger. I was proud of you. You helped catch a bad guy. I think you're wonderful. Strong, confident, smart. We make a good team, whether it's in the OR, catching criminals and when making love. I don't care who knows how I feel about you."

"But you didn't have to kiss me."

"I didn't plan it if that's what you're wanting to know. It was pure emotion on my part, and I'm not sorry I did it. You might not want to hear this or you might throw it back in my face and I won't blame you after the way I've treated you, but I kissed you because I realized I love you. I was so afraid for you when Mark went into your OR. Dale had to stop me from following Mark in, which might have tipped him off. I paced the unit floor until it was all over. I was terrified something would happen to you."

Valerie sat straighter, her head turned and she was listening intently. "What did you say a few words back?"

"That I was scared for you?"

She slowly shook her head. "No, just before that."

"That I love you."

"Yeah, that." A smile formed on her lips.

He moved so he could take one of her hands. "I do love you. I just hope I haven't destroyed what feelings you had for me."

Before he could take a breath, Valerie was in his arms giving him a tender kiss that had him daring to hope she might feel the same about him.

"I love you too."

He pulled her close and sealed the moment with another kiss. One that soon turned to passion. He nudged her away. "I have more to say before I can't stand it any longer and ask if I can take you to bed. It needs to be said. I want you to have no doubts about my feelings for you.

"I did you wrong the day after we made love. My only excuse is that I was running. I was running from my guilt, from my true feelings and my fear of how life had changed since you truly entered it. I think there must've been something more there even before we went to the wedding because you were the only person I considered taking with me. I think my feelings have run deep for you for a long time, and I just refused to open my eyes.

"I want you to know if you'll give me another chance that I'll never choose anyone over you. I'll never leave your side. You're the most important person in my life. In fact, you are my life. If I've learned anything in these last two miserable weeks of not having you in my arms, not kissing you, it is that I don't enjoy life without you. You brought me back to life just as surely as if you had resuscitated me.

"I've treated you badly. I know I don't deserve you, but I promise to always stand by you. I'll try to never let you down. If you'll give me another chance, I'll do my best to be the man you need. I do love you, and I always will."

Valerie cupped his cheek and kissed him softly.

"I've never heard a more perfect speech and I have one as well. Over the last few days you have stood by me. You disrupted your life to make sure I was safe. That's more than any other man has ever done. You've shown me more by your actions than anyone ever has in words what a special man you are. Even at the wedding, more than once you protected me, stood beside me. You are who I've been looking for all my life."

Owen pulled her into his lap and kissed her soundly.

"Do you remember back when you had us asking questions so we could get to know each other?"

Valerie nodded.

"I said I wanted to wait to ask you something because I didn't know what to ask. Well, I've thought of my question."

She grinned. "I already know your spirit animal."

"I'm not going to ask my question if you don't stop making fun of me."

Valerie straightened her face. "Go ahead. I'm listening."

"My question is, will you marry me?"

Her eyes widened, and her mouth dropped open. Her arms tightened around his neck. "Yes, my love. I can't think of anything I want more."

* * * * *

*If you missed the previous story
in the Atlanta Children's Hospital trilogy,
then check out*

Reunited with the Children's Doc

*And if you enjoyed this story, check out
these other great reads from Susan Carlisle*

Mending the ER Doc's Heart
From Florida Fling to Forever
Taming the Hot-Shot Doc

All available now!